THE MAN FROM YORKSHIRE©

A Novella

E. WAINDECKER

Reader reviews: ~

"Fascinating! This is an intriguing book! There's certainly an element of mystery: Was Eric murdered or did he die of natural causes? Was he involved in nefarious international dealings or was he just a regular guy? Perhaps most interesting is the historical context which the author weaves into her story....."

"The most compelling book I've read in a very long time!!! The Man from Yorkshire was an extremely compelling read. It was such a page turner that I found myself reading it over 3 times. Every time I read it another nuance was discovered. The characters were real for me..."

"From the first page it put me in a nice nostalgic mood. Erika WainDecker can always be counted on for a very entertaining book... or in this case a novella. From the first page it put me in a nice nostalgic mood, with a historical setting told in a perfect tone. In my mind's eye the story was unfolding in black and white, like a classic movie. An excellent read.

THE MAN FROM YORKSHIRE©

~ A Novella ~

E. WainDecker

THE MAN FROM YORKSHIRE

Dog Day Publisher/2015
November

All rights reserved

Copyright © 2015 by E. WainDecker

Cover illustration © 2015 by E. WainDecker

ISBN-13: 978-1494854454

ISBN-10: 1494854457

THE MAN FROM YORKSHIRE

~ A Novella ~

E.WainDecker

The Old Finishes ~
A New one Begins

~ ~ ~ ~

THE MILLENIUM was birthed in a sea of fireworks visible around the world. People cheered and welcomed in their new player. Their new future.
And as Wikipedia stated, "The "year 2000" has also been a popular phrase referring to an often Utopian future, or a year when stories in such a future were set, adding to its cultural significance. There was also media and public interest in the Y2Kbug ~ a problem for both digital (computer-related) and non-digital documentation and data storage situations which resulted from the practice of abbreviating a four-digit year to two digits.
This made year 2000 indistinguishable from 1900. The former assumption that a twentieth-century date was always understood caused various errors concerning, in particular, the display of dates and the automated ordering of dated records or real-time events. Firstly, the practice of representing the year with two digits becomes problematic with logical error(s) arising upon "rollover" from x99 to x00. This has caused some date-related processing to operate incurrectly for dates and times on and after 1 January 2000, and on other critical dates which were billed 'event horizons.' Without corrective action, long-working systems would break down when the "... 97, 98, 99, 00 ..." ascending numbering assumption suddenly became invalid.
"Secondly, some programmers had misunderstood the rule that determines whether years that are exactly divisible by 100 are not leap years, and assumed the year 2000 would not be a leap year. Although most years divisible by 100 are not leap years, if they are divisible by 400 then they are. Thus the year 2000 was a leap year.

"Companies and organizations worldwide checked, fixed, and upgraded their computer systems. Thus, the populist argument was that the new millennium should begin when the zeroes "rolled over" to 2000, i.e. the day after December 31, 1999. People felt that the change of hundred digit in the year number, and the zeros rolling over, created a sense that a new century had begun. This is similar to the common demarcation of decades by their most significant digits, e.g. naming the period 1980 to 1989 as the 1980s or "the eighties". Similarly, it would be valid to celebrate the year 2000 as a cultural event in its own right, and name the period 2000 to 2999 as "the 2000s"."

Enough. Suffice to say we have arrived ~

I have been sitting here on the living room floor of my hillside house for hours. Moby tunes fill the air ~ transcending music for the occasion. A tall glass of white wine, Moscatto, sweet for an afternoon, and a few banana cake strips help me comb through boxes and boxes of old scrap-books, news papers, documents, and pictures that my mother, Charlotte, had saved. Everything and anything that chronicled my father is just now under review, as prior to this time, nothing was made privy to me. Odd, come to think of it, very odd as I am now in my mid sixties. My mother was a very private woman in many ways. What was there that needed guarding? My father perhaps? A mystery. I take a sip of wine and fork a thin slice of bread.

Charlotte died three years ago at the ripe old age of 98. She had long outlived not only my first father, whose information I am now sifting through but a second, followed by a third. My father's funeral had been held at the Anglican Church in the small suburb township outside Montreal proper, St. Lambert, now home to the yuppie 30's with families and riches from new internet money. All readying to retire shortly. How odd. The church had been so packed that the mourners spilled outward, down the steps on to the sidewalk. They had come from all over the world. Black limousines lined the curbs while attending chauffeurs in black suits stood at attention by their doors. The casket had been open, as was the fashion then.

Nowadays cremation through Neptune Society is the way to go. A small canister in a coloured party bag is handed to the bereaved – the sum of one's physical corporeal life, reduced by fire, encased in a small and seemingly unimportant everyday canister with a lid that one struggles to remove. I found this out when my husband of 30 years died. My daughter, Grace, and I went to pick up the ashes.

The visit to the Neptune office was quite surreal, to say the least, as we returned with a party favour bag, our choice of colour, mind you, filled with his remains. In hand. In a bag. So odd. So odd.

I'm Emma. Emma James Charles. I married Chandler Charles after attending McGill University, following in my father's footsteps, and got my degree in architectural urban planning. Chandler was a businessman from Halifax who visited and stayed, joining CIL, Canadian Industries Limited, as head financial manager for World Operations. We raised a daughter, Grace Claire, who married a young South American diplomat whom she met at a dinner party. Tomatio Estoya, the great-grandson of Raoul and Souetes Estoya, my father's best friends. The seedlings didn't fall far from the tree, as they say.

And now, just now, I am finally able to review the many boxes that have been stacked high in the corner where they had been neatly put after my mother's death. So many boxes, so much stuff for me to sift through. Charlotte kept every thing. I found myself enthralled. I took a sip of wine and a taste of the banana bread and thought how interesting to see one's history unfold into another's present. Their scrapbooks of places I myself have visited, even to some of the very same sites, even the very same hotels, now restored and done over for my time. Some pictures taken from the very same vantage points. How similar in mind and thought. Funny.

Dad had died when I was a child of ten, much too young for any true awareness of just who he was or what kind of man he actually might have been. I knew him through a child's eyes, a well loved father who was there when he was, considering his business took heavy demands of his time, weighing in heftily. He was a macha macha, as the term goes. A big Kuana. He was my father. Dad.

The man who gave me my much prized FAO Schwartz, New York City, pogo stick in shinny aluminium steel with a series of heavily bound springy coils that ran up the centre of the stick, bordered by two gridded foot rests - truly the envy of the neighbourhood children. I could make over a hundred jumps per use – high jumps at that. The cowgirl boots and outfit from Saks Fifth Avenue, the Danielle Boone cap, my Captain's hat for beach days ~ countless other wonders that stay strong in my memory. The times I watched him with his train set that he had so diligently built in the basement on a large working table with lights and whistles and little people and station houses with dogs and paperboys and trees and snow.

The tiny neon fish whose bony spines appeared to illuminate as they swam around the aquarium located in a corner of the wood panelled dinning room - the same kind of fish that I and Grace later sought out for our aquarium. I have taken much from a man I knew nothing about other than what he was like as a father. He was the magician at parties who surprised us with inter-locked rings and rabbits in hats. The glass spinner who created wondrous music from filled and partially filled glasses of water.

The zilaphone player who quickly and energetically bounced his padded sticks over the metal keyboard creating lively sounds. The artist who had made a living doing posters while at college and who spent every summer at Cape Cod lost in watercolours. The chef who was master of his outdoor Bar-BQ built of brick. The man with the lampshade atop his head. His laugh. His happy face. Always happy. The man from Yorkshire.

I placed pictures into two piles ~ those I would hang up in frames and those I would simply pin up on the wall in the office around the worktable, the computer throne. The house pictures of where I had grown up. The business pictures of my father riding the Canadian Railway, official government flags blowing in the breeze, while he and his business minion sat at the window talking and plotting the fate of what, I was not sure. Then there was the intriguing picture of him with the small camera, his hat pushed up at the brim, as he squinted, clicking away with the chemical plant as backdrop. The spy camera as we now call it. One that a James Bond character might use. Small enough to hold in the palm of one's hand, undetectable and certainly not available to the public at the time of his ownership. I looked and wondered. What had the old dog been up to?

He had been everywhere when everything was happening. When history was being made. Always looking well put together, tidy and intelligent, a sharp dresser at all times, even at home when gardening with his cigarette dangling from his lips, shirt sleeves rolled up under his traditional suspenders, and his small glassed *neat*

Scotch. Always working on something. The machinery was always working.

And the pictures of my mother and father standing together on the ocean liner's deck. The stateroom filled with bouquets of flowers with greetings from people from all over the world. It felt as though I was forever waving goodbye at the dock, streamers flying through the air, cascading downward over the railings into the water below, as the gang plank was being removed and the ship slowly moved off into the big ocean to cross to the other side of the world.

Nothing quite like traveling by boat, then. Large steamer trunks that opened outward, meticulously hand sewn silk lined interiors, complete with hangers for expectant dresses and suits, little cubbies for everything else. All those white trunks pasted in stickers from around the world. Mexico, Argentina, Brazil, London, Paris, Germany, Switzerland, Cairo, just to name a few. And then those same trunks returned to their cedar panelled trunk room, especially built just for them, to await their next adventure. If only those trunks could speak. What tales. What images. Imagine having a trunk room. Such times.

Grace would probably find all of this interesting if she wasn't so busy with her job, outside interests, and life in general. She is now living in Ottawa, the seat of government, with her husband, Tomatio Estoya, diplomat to South America. I am sure his post was in part due to his brilliance in negotiation and in part due to his grandparents, Raoul and Souetes. My parent's greatest friends who were themselves very influential in the political arena.

Her international law degree has come in handy. She speaks French and several other languages. Great Grandmother Lily would be pleased. The need for knowledge runs deep in this family. CSIS/ The Canadian Security Intelligence Services – to the French the SCRS /Service Canadien du Renseignement de Securite were thrilled to have her on board. And as the CSIS/SCRS work closely with Quadpartie Pact, a post WWII shared agency with United States, UK and Australia, and now the CCIRC, Canadian Cyber Incident Response Centre, her services are in constant demand. She has proven herself to be indispensible. Her grandfather would have been very proud of her.

I certainly am.

I took a sip of wine and reflected on the box before me. I

continued to dig through the volumes of material and wondered why I had waited so long. It was now many years since my mother's death. Charlotte had left her mark on everyone. I was not spared. I came across a small envelope stuffed inside the back cover of one of the scrapbooks. I only noticed it because I had been running my hand across the cover. The leather had a slight bulge, not really visible to the eye but certainly to the touch. I pulled out the tiny envelope and found a small key. Nothing more. The key. It looked like something that might fit a box, perhaps one of those my parents always had on the mantle library or on a shelf. I decided to find the owner so I put down the scrapbook and started to look around the room. I had kept all of the boxes I thought of interest, as most were inlaid with ivory or shell or with some exotic wood. My father was very fond of boxes and I guess I have simply kept the tradition ongoing. After an hour of checking everything and everywhere I finally found that the key fit a long ornate box, mother of pearl shell inlay, with a rounded top. The key not only fit the lock but actually turned it as well. Often keys fit other slots but do not turn hence wrong key ~ but this one did.

    I turned the key ever so slowly as not to damage the old wood. The top opened with a click. I waited a moment, not sure, not wanting to intrude where I ought not to go, but then considered the find and the situation itself. I raised the lid and saw a beautifully crafted interior complete with matching red velvet lining top and bottom. There was actually little in the box, a few ribbons and buttons. The sides were puffy with an obvious filled lining. Perhaps a sewing box. But why the key? Odd for a sewing box, I thought. Very odd. I felt the sides and the bottom thinking a 'secret passage' and again to my surprise my fingers ran across a raised area. I pulled at the side of the material and gently pealed it back. A note pad was hiding, waiting to be found with its story to be told. I held my breath for a moment. I took another sip of wine. Then I removed the little note pad and opened the flip top.

    Inside were the letters "TTF". I looked at them blankly. They meant nothing to me. TTF, written in my mother's handwriting. But what did it mean? And again she had written:

> *To live for the time period allotted by the life span – to experience everything as it would be.*
> *To die and then be suspended in energy until a new was found.*

> *Transmitting the information through ~*
> *encompassing all from the beginning to the end*
> *in one endless ripple. Seamlessly.*

I read the words over and over again; still not sure I understood their meaning. Was she talking about a concept, a person, a thing, an event? The second page had a quote, possibly from a book. I wasn't sure. I thought Cloud Atlas and wondered.

> *Our lives are not our own*
> *From womb to tomb*
> *We are bound to others*
> *Past and present and by*
> *Each crime*
> *Each kindness...*
> *Makes both our future*

I paused and tried to think what the connection could be. Why these quotes? Why these words? To whom? About whom? For whom? I flipped the pages. There was nothing else written for several pages and then another scribbling. *I knew something was different. Lily had said it from the start. He was different. And his own words," I have lived such a long life."* But ~ Again several pages of nothing and then more writing.

He has to be protected. Lily told me to be on my watch. He had great things to do. Things we might not understand or perhaps were not meant to. They will be looking for him, Lily said. They will kill him.

What was she talking about? Kill? Who? My father had died of a brain rupture. That's what we were told. Outside the Ritz Carlton Hotel. Who would have killed him? For what reason? I put the note pad down momentarily and tried to get a sense of perspective here.

Get a sense of understanding as to why Charlotte would have thought and/or even written this. I took another sip of wine and walked through the room into the drawing room with the note pad in my hand, leaving the box open and the key dangling from the top.

I walked to the window seat and sat down, opening the small note pad once again, I flipped through the pages to another set of words neatly written but with no reference, just words and letters. It was clear that homework was going to be required. Reading the words again I jotted them down on a spare piece of paper so as not to change

13

or destroy the original pad. It was time to go to the computer and play catch up.

    SOE
    Operation Pedestal
    Oslo Report
    Diamonds
    CIS – CRS

~ ~ ~ ~ ~

    SOE referred to British WWII organization officially formed by the Minister of Economic Warfare High Dalton back in July 1940. The purpose was to conduct espionage and sabotage, reconnaissance in then occupied Europe, to aid local resistance movements against the Axis powers. Originally to be activated in the event of a German invasion of British shores. Few people were even aware of the SOE's existence. Sometimes referred as the Baker Street Irregulars, their location being headquartered in London. I had heard the *Baker Street Irregulars* name several times as a child when Mr. Gently and my father would chat over a drink at the bar cleverly designed as a private and secret room off the formal dining room itself. Dad had had it constructed when he built the house. I thought it was some men's club. Funny. In actuality it was known as Churchill's Secret Army hence the coined name Ministry of Ungentlemanly Warfare.

    Sanctioned to operate in all countries including former countries attacked or occupied by the Axis forces, offering neutral territory on occasion. Incredibly it employed just over 13,000 people, 3,200 women, and it supplied about 1,000,000 operatives worldwide. Officially it was dissolved January 15, 1944. Although my father was too old for military action itself then, I remember seeing pictures of him with a business group taking meetings with Churchill. Could it be that he was himself one of those *ungentlemanly* gentlemen? Always there. There, where the action was.

    Operation Pedestal was another British operation getting well needed supplies to the island of Malta in 1942, during WWII. Malta was the base for submarines, aircraft and surface ships that attacked the Axis convoys carrying supplies to both the Italian and German armies based in North Africa. And for that Malta was heavily under siege. To sustain the base the UK had to get their convoys through at all costs so the SS OHIO, an American built-joint Greek enterprise, apparently part of shipping magnate Aris Nassi's arsenal, sailed through the Strait of Gibraltar with its British crew. The day was the Feast of the Assumption (Santa Marija), August 15, 1942.

Apparently there was an incredible run of fifty ships that past E-boats, bombers submarines and minefields. Considered one of the more important British strategic victories of WWII. The death toll was high as only five of the original fifteen merchant ships ever reached the Grand Harbour. Even today and every August 15th, *the event* has become synonymous with the public holiday celebrations. Malta. The colourful stickers plastered onto those pristine cream trunk surfaces clearly crying out Malta. He had been there. My father had been connected. But the trunk room had long since been dismantled unfortunately. The trunks themselves sold to collectors. Then the house and then we had moved. There would be no further trace.

The Oslo Report was one of those spectacular leaks in military intelligence. Hans Ferdinand Mayer, German mathematician and physicist, had written a report during a business trip to Oslo, Norway in November 1939. Telecommunications being a passion of his, Mayer had joined Siemens AG in 1922. The company had built the first ever long-distance telegraph line in Europe with branches throughout Europe and of course one in London which dated back to 1850. Others were in Russia also dating back to 1855. The main branches obviously were in Berlin and Munich. Mayer became director in 1936, hence giving him contacts all over Europe and United States. But just after Hitler's invasion into Poland in September 1939, an action which so inflamed and revolted his sensibilities, Mayer sought to take action against the Axis power.

With the aid of an operative, no name given, to broker a meet with Ronnie Gently in Norway, both men checked into the Hotel Bristol. That was October 1939. On a borrowed typewriter from the hotel, Mayer typed a *personal* letter asking the British military attaché, a friend of Raoul Estoya, to alter the German language programme then airing on the BBC World Service. This would serve as a sign of interest and acceptance.

There was again mention of the shipping magnate, Aris Nassi, who while checking on his tankers had met up with a Ronnie Gently in early October. The same Mr. Gently who dined at the house and who I would playfully call *Uncle Ronnie*. The reputed report described German weapons current and to come. Mayer then mailed his report, anonymously, as two separate *personal* letters to the British Embassy in Oslo, who in turn passed them on to MI6 in London for analysis. The result was an invaluable resource for counter measure re: Navigational and Targeting Radars.

Done, he then sent a follow-up to his report with a proximity fuse, an actual fuse that could detonate an explosive device automatically when a target passed another or the target became smaller than predetermined. The Mark 53 was one such fuse. Depending largely on the development of such a radar for victory, an incredible technological innovation to be sure was what Mayer was giving to the British willingly. What a coup.

Henry Turner, a friend of Huber Johnston, my father's mentor and liaison, was to handle communication via their Danish colleague, Niels Hoomblad. I remember the names as Charlotte and my father mentioned them, in passing of course. At the time they were just names bouncing off a child's ear. Denmark was then neutral and Mayer travelled to see Niels. But Hitler invaded Denmark so the communication route was severed. Sadly, when Mayer returned to Germany, he was arrested and imprisoned in a concentration camp until the war's end. The Oslo Report was never exposed to the Nazis, but without the information the tide would have or certainly could have been very different. The contribution of Mayer and the connectives through which he was able to share the information certainly contributed to the turning point in the fight against the Axis powers. All of this was informational ~ history, now.

I paused. The man from Yorkshire had been connected to everything and everyone either through association with or management of. How extraordinary. How incredible. I didn't understand. I wasn't sure if I wanted to understand.

CHAPTER one ~

The cold, wet night air slapped my face hard as I stepped out of the Ritz Carlton Hotel onto a now quiet Sherbrooke Street. I pulled my white silk scarf up around my neck, adjusted my newly purchased hat from Holt Renfrew, nice brim with silk hat-band, collared my long black wool winter coat and pulled on my soft gray calf skin gloves. I liked to dress up and clothes always looked good on me. I had decided to walk the block or two to the cabbie. Always thought it a waste of gas to drive back to the suburbs by myself and tonight I would enjoy that moment of leisure time, watching the snow fall, hearing the crunch of the granular particles under my boots now readily blanketing the pavement. The evening events had gone smoothly and the speech had been well accepted and enjoyed, I thought. The Convention of Purchasing Agents for the Commonwealth had once again been realized and I had been awarded highest honours. I smiled enjoying that knowledge. And then it hit me.

My mouth went dry and my face fell away. I felt my vocal cords and muscles swell up and chock my esophagus. No words to utter. A man of words now silenced. The sudden indescribable zing, followed by a pulsating thunder inside my head, deafening my ears. My legs crumbled like match sticks gone up in flame. A heat seared through my eyes and the shock to my system sent me tumbling to the ground without so much as a whimper or cry out. It was all so damn fast and out of the blue, as Charlotte would have said. Out of the blue. It was a cerebral thrombosis. She would be told later as both she and our daughter had gone to the Laurentians for one of our winter wonderland ski trips. They were joined by the Hutchisons and Elberts and I was to join later. I guess I wouldn't be, not this time round. I'm sure the black limousine would pull up to the lodge and the men in black would escort my Charlotte and Emma to the car for the long trip back to the house. The cerebral thrombosis would be the official story but the Humints knew the truth. One clean shot. Execution.

17

I could feel the cold snow under my chin as my head hit the ground. A melon cracking. Time has a way of stopping, I had heard, and it was true, freezing the moment like film on the reel spool. It would have been instantaneous, she would be told, but for me, it was a panorama of my life that flashed through that instant, locked in time, before my essence faded and melted into the snow, another casualty of a life well spent. And it was. I knew it but ~ the white ~ the cold ~

I grew up in Yorkshire in eighteen ninety-five. Just before the turn of the century. As I was to say in an interview years later, "I have lived a very long time."

Bradford, Yorkshire – a textile town. It was a boomtown of the Industrial Revolution and amongst the earliest industrialized settlements ~ the wool capital of the world. The area itself accessed coal and iron ore, and soft water facilitated the growth of Bradford's manufacturing base.

We were in the Northern part of England, a metropolitan borough of West Yorkshire. A city of sandstone. The soft water involved the removal of calcium, magnesium and other metals. This was done using ion-exchange resins ~ *I thought that interesting.*

Bradford had become a destination for immigrants starting with the Irish in the 1840's (long before me, of course) and then by the late 1890's the Germans and Jewish immigrants and merchants, like Jacob Behrens who exported woolen goods, having developed his company into an international multi-million pound business. Worsted spinners like Lister's Mill – Samuel Lister suggesting capitalist attitudes making trade unions necessary. Problems with factories churning out clouds of black smoke, black sulfurous smoke due to the unprecedented growth. ~ *Times were a changing and changing fast at the turn of the century ~*

Bradford had become one of the most polluted cities in the UK. England. Machinery bases grew up to support the textiles and this led to diversification - cars, the Jowett Motor Company established at the turn of the century by the two Jowett boys, William and Benjamin, with partner Arthur Lamb. Bradford was humming despite the extremely high levels of infant and youth mortalities ~ frequent outbreaks of cholera and typhoid. Only 30% of textile worker children reached the age of fifteen. Life expectancy of Bradford residents was just over eighteen years, which was one of the lowest in the country.

~ Harsh times ~ Interesting times.
   I lived there with my mother, Lily James, my sister, Ethel and brother Jack. I was the last of the three. I bore my father's name, Eric James. My father had died when I was quite young. He worked in the mines, so I was told. Frankly I didn't remember him but both Ethel and Jack kept the stories alive so at times I actually thought I remembered both him and the events that happened. Of course, I didn't but it felt good, all the same. Thinking I did.
   We lived in a row house, small but always neat. My mother gardened for sustainable food supplies ~ crops that rotated throughout the year. Not much space but enough to keep us above ground, as it were. We all tended the long thin garden section with pride and enthusiasm. After all, Benjamin Rabbit might come a wandering through and without ol' farmer John to whisk him away, well. Though I was taught to share and share alike, as one never could know when the tables might turn. Not sure how that applied to Benjamin Rabbit but I liked the concept.
   My mother worked houses, as kitchen and laundry help. She was a smart, well visioned woman. Long auburn hair tied in a knot ~ always elegant and feminine. Not harsh looking or harsh in manner. She may have come from country stock and worked a menial job, as one might see it now, but she was always proud of her day's work. Always a delight to see and hear. A mellifluous voice like that of an angel, so the saying goes. I admired her as a person and liked her as a mother. But she was not one to cross. Oh no. Not one to cross.
   My sister, Ethel, had proven herself to be quite the sport person and had offers to swim in competitions. She was a clever woman destined for great things. Jack was an adept musician, the fiddle, and had aspirations of being an entrepreneur, somewhere, some day. Life was what it was and as long as we were all together it didn't really matter if we had or had not. We worked it out. I really don't remember too much about the actual living of it ~ odd I'm sure some might say or think but that's simply the way it was. I rose in the morning, went to school, came home and played with my mates on the street, ate dinner and went to bed.
   My chums, Teddy and Robbie, and I would play down at the old Victorian Wool Exchange building, a triangular sort of building situated at the corner, a cross roads to a future. The oldest building

19

was the cathedral, better known as our parish church. And there was Bolling Hall, a grand building from medieval times, which ultimately became a museum. The large Victorian cemetery at Undercliffe was our favourite place to adventure. How we loved to gallivant like little horses through the grounds, looking at the headstones, reading the inscriptions and imagining tall tales of ghostly stories. And then there was always time for The Victorian Hotel and the Midland Hotel, both built to accommodate the business travellers during the height of the wool trade. Large lounge rooms with expansive wooden Desk fronts, as I would come to know these and even someday return to take my rightful place in the suites offered to the rich and powerful. The rich and powerful. All so relative.

I had just addressed that issue in my speech, *"...despite my needing to make you all aim to be super P. A.'s there may be many who just don't want to make the effort, not because they are lazy or lack initiative, but because they are happy where they are. This is as it should be – we can't all be on top of the pile at the same time. So let's look at this matter philosophically. My own personal definition of a completely successful man is one who is happy at home, happy in his job, and who can sleep well. On this basis you will find a far greater percentage of successful men in the lower ranks than at the presidential level – and I am not including presidency in associations such as this.*

"Some of you will have already arrived at this point. I have and to those and myself I say 'Congratulations'. "Nevertheless, there are still a large number among us to whom competition is the spice of life – out of these will come our leaders." ~ Not bad for a small town boy.

But for now, Teddy and I would offer our services as errand boys. The pay was better than not and the Desk people pleasant. Robbie wasn't allowed to work. It was beneath him.

I schooled at Bradford Grammar School, in existence near the parish church since the mid-16th century. It was then re-established by Royal Charter as the Free Grammar School of Charles II somewhere around 1667. Our University was actually founded in the 1860's as the Bradford Schools of Weaving, Design and Building. Courses included technology and management science, medical sciences, nursing studies, optometry pharmacy, modern languages and archaeology. My mother had lofty ideas that we would all go to higher schooling when the time came. I was never quite sure how that would happen as schooling was costly and there was a hierarchy within the class structure, whether we liked it or not. But at this point in my life, I pushed such thoughts to the back. I studied hard, as education was a strong point in the household.

Without self-education there was nowhere for a person to go – no way to rise above his or her given rank. Education was the key. Lily saw to it that we understood her primary rule for success.

And then there were the wonderful holiday outings when we would go to Brighton ~ it emerged as a health resort featuring Sea Bathing during the 18th century and became a destination for day-trippers from London and other parts after the arrival of the railway in 1841. I remember taking my wife Charlotte there for one of our early anniversaries. I had hoped she might like it. I don't think she did but it brought back such warm memories of my youth. Those outings were very special. Funny now to think that 'back then' resorts promoted the purported health benefits of seawater as if it were something extraordinary. After all it was water, just water, salty water. Then there were dippers, guides as to how to enjoy the bathing machines ~ a sort of wagon which sat at the water's edge. One would be escorted down the stairs into the waters to dip, immerse themselves ~ the standard dip was considered three total immersions. This actual practice of dipping with assistance was made famous with Martha Gunn and Old Smoaker of Brighton both reported to have worked for the Prince Regent himself and of course, this was a thing of the past, when I was a boy, but I did hear about it and the wagons still stand and funnily enough have taken on a new life on European beaches as bathing boxes, now commonly called *cabanas*. ~ *Life recycles ~ taking something old, giving it a new twist.*

Sister Ethel was always offered a job as lifeguard during the tourist season. And one must understand that for a woman this was extraordinary, to say the least. In fact, my sister Ethel will always be considered a most unusual, non-conformist individual by most people, if not all. A person out of sync with her own time. One so far advanced in her thinking of life and mores with regards women and their role and placement in life and society, as a whole. I always thought of her as my role model for my appreciation of women.

Women in general. ~ *I drift* ~ *I did so love to swim. Cape Cod with Charlotte and our daughter Emma in the summer* ~ *Horn Cottages. I guess someone else will use our space now. My space.*

We left Bradford one day, packed up all our belongings into several suitcases and headed for a new land, across the sea. My mother said Bradford could only lead us to the mills or mines and neither was good enough. We left before the summer heat exploded, and before the fall leaves began turning. It was a sign of change and Lily James was all about signs of change.

We moved to Montreal when I was eleven. That was 1906. It would prove to be an exciting city. We had been given a contact person there from one of the families for whom my mother had worked. Boat passage had been steerage located at the bottom level. Crammed in with all the other immigrants, a sea of languages, cultures, peoples and aromas. The latter, nicely phrased. Our immediate food supplies ran out quickly but with a little bartering here and there we landed on the new shore none the worse for wear.

Certainly better than some. Less than others. But there was a future ahead, as Lily would see to that. We took a small house in NDG. Notre-Dame-de-Grace. In the 1660s, three families Décarie, Hurtubise and Milot originally from the new colony of Ville Marie became landowners in the area known as Coteau Saint-Pierre. The Village of Notre-Dame-de-Grâce established in 1876 grew rapidly thanks to its rural ambiance. Because of its fertile soil apples and melons, cabbages, tomatoes and onions were produced, leading to the apples being shipped to England and the melons being highly prized in New York (Waldorf Astoria), The Windsor Hotel in Montreal and throughout Boston. The Elmhurst Dairy, founded in the late 1870s, increased its grazing land by 400 acres in the subsequent years, even before NDG was incorporated as a town in 1906, obviously my mother chose an auspicious time as change was in the air everywhere. The town was later annexed by the City of Montreal as the NDG ward in 1910, the same year Leon Belec gave up his office as the first police and fire chief. His ancestry ran back 175 years, originating in Brittany, with his mother being a Prud'-homme descendant.

By 1914, there were 5,000 inhabitants, and by 1930, their numbers had increased to 30,000. ~ *All of this according to the history books on Montreal, I remember reading, and the stories told and retold to me by my mother and Ethel* ~ None of which was lost on my mother, Lily James, the gardener - that and her love for the wooden porch buildings, which were considered the best of all the neighbourhoods.

Apparently at the beginning of the century there had been a devastating frost so Anatole Decarie, melon grower, was approached by a Montreal restaurateur questioning where it would be possible to replace his fresh melon on the desert menu with Mme. Decarie's fast becoming famous melon jam. The Decarie kitchen became a small factory. The Windsor Hotel enjoyed the aromas of the pungent jams. And Lily James joined the work force in the kitchen.

It is said that Barthelemy Thelesphore Decarie actually started the culture of muskmelons from seed brought back from France by an employee cultivating the lands from St. Jacques to Cote St. Luc. The Declarie family had had the land since 1675. The NDG melons were even enjoyed by King Edward VII at Buckingham Palace. Boxes specially ordered bore the name of Anatole Decarie, his occupation "cultivatuer" and his address. Such history. Such hope. NDG was truly a borough to be reckoned with. It would only be a few years later that the first tramway would make its appearance in Notre-Dame-de-Grace, taking off from Mount Royal Street, around the mountain and terminating at Snowdon Station. All of this in 1908. NDG. Tree-lined streets, brick houses, closely cropped duplexes, wooden porches.

Life was interesting. Truly interesting. The city centre itself, old Montreal, Vieux Ville, was bustling with commerce. The seaport was thriving with ships coming in and out of the harbor. Regular life wasn't much different – school, chores, playing, sleeping. Ethel who was five years older, now sixteen, had enrolled in Montreal High School.

She had always been a good student and she was looking to go to McGill University, as they had a very good physical education program. She wanted to teach sports and of course, to excel herself. She actually did both, becoming one of the top fencers. She was very popular on the University campus despite her peculiar thoughts and ways. Not that I thought her odd but for most people, she was.

And frankly Ethel could have cared less. She was her own

person. And later she would take her place among the women who sought equality as women in a man's world.

Ethel befriended Emily Murphy, the prominent suffragette and reformer who was appointed Police Magistrate in 1916, actually the first female in the Commonwealth. Britain was still our 'Mother' sovereign - we were a loose and voluntary association, about one-quarter of the world's population mostly of former colonies, 54 independent nations, pledging to co-operate and consult in furthering world peace, racial equality and economic development. All lofty ideals but in truth, held under the 'Mother's thumb. Emily Murphy went on to write books and articles under the nom de plume Janey Canuck. Ethel and she were close despite their age difference.

And then there was Henrietta Muir Edwards who advocated mother's allowances, equal parental rights and divorce, among other issues. She published **Working Women of Canada,** Canada's first magazine for women. And not to forget Agnes MacPhail, CCF MP, and Canada's First Canadian Member of Parliament who worked prison reform and old age pensions. Such were the friends and interactions of my sister, Ethel, right in step with her time and yet so far ahead.

When the Great War of 1914 began, Ethel volunteered to help out the Allied Powers. And being female, the military did not allow combat positions, though I know she would have taken one and been damn good at it, she applied, instead, as ambulance driver in France. She was twenty-four. She would return and graduate when the war was finished. When her term was done. *~ Funnily, I always remember her encounters with some interesting people ~ Rene Clair and Jean Cocteau, film makers, Betty Carstairs, a wealthy Anglo-American power boat racer who was as eclectic as she, and Helene Dutrieu, a pioneer French aviator. Then there was Ralph Vaughan Williams and Maurice Ravel. "The music doesn't stop." She said. I laugh. Ethel did have a way with people ~*

We were all to be labeled The Lost Generation by returning writers. Lost by the years taken from our lives. Unfortunately some who returned never really did, just in body and some not even in that. But both my sister and I were lucky. And once home we never talked about the Great War to End All Wars, as it was called. *~ The GREAT War for Civilization. Surely it would never happen again.*

~ the cold snow is fresh on my skin. I think of the old port.
    Jack had turned fourteen and he also attended Montreal High. Not an exceptional student though good enough. His interests were always varied. Nothing set. Always searching. And when the time came, he chose not to go to McGill but instead left for Toronto, Queens University. In 1911, the Faculty of Theology decided to separate from the rapidly growing university (Queen's became secular in 1912 - the Presbyterian Church in Canada obtained a Royal Charter from Queen Victoria, a Presbyterian.) On April 1, 1912, Queen's Theological College was created by an Act of Parliament, complete with its own Board of Management. Jack was right in time with change. The course of study he had chosen suited him well and he went on for graduate studies in Restorative Justice. That's a focus on the needs of the victims and their offenders, and any involved community, instead of abstract legal practices being satisfied, and wrongdoers punished. The thought was to encourage responsibility of one's actions, fostering dialogue between victim and offender ~ returning stolen property, serving community time, the simple act of giving an apology. Our mother had taught us well in management of the human condi-tion and how to serve it.
    Jack chose not to serve in the war, the Great War *that would end all wars* sweeping across Europe in 1914. But he did his part on the home front with returning men and women, giving counseling and service where needed and asked for by the government. We were proud of him. He was married by then to a Hamilton girl. Jack was twenty-four and Reina was nineteen. A good match. She thought he was the cat's pajamas. Never was quite sure what that actually meant as cats in pajamas wasn't a visual that I had witnessed. Suffice to say, she thought he was the end all. Jack died in 1949. Just dropped one day. Reina then joined her sister, Violet, a slight, very elegant Victorian styled woman who never married. More's the pity as she was a wonderful cook and had a marvelous sense of humour. She probably scared men away with her ease, charm and intelligence.
    Reina, on the other hand, was the total opposite. She was large and brutish in appearance, but not so in nature. ~ *Always reminded my daughter Emma of Toady from Toad Hall*. Large, robust.
    Opposites certainly do attract. Jack and Reina. But they fit like peas in a pod. And then one day he just dropped ~ *and here I lie in*

the cold snow. Dropped like a bundle of match sticks burning out. Not out yet.

When I heard of the war and the need for men I enlisted without telling anyone. I was nineteen. I had finished Montreal High following in the James' footsteps having been very active in debate and sports and living life. I even wrote for the school newspaper ~ *I still do for The Gazette. No, that would be – I did. Past tense, very soon.*

Our mother was not pleased to be loosing two of her children to the war operation overseas but she knew that she had raised us with awareness for history and this was history in the making. We knew she would continue with life and that our Victory Garden would become her symbol of endurance. Ethel and I also knew we would be returning as we had things to do. Life to be played out. Jack was on home ground and that was comforting. Lily continued on.

So Ethel and I moved out together aboard the steam liner for the other side of the world, again. We would never actually come into contact with each other while we were there, on the front, but word of mouth was sent round, from time to time, like jungle drums beating their timeless message, the tireless arms beating their palms to the skins.

I found myself in the thick of it. I was infantry. The trenches. I kept a diary – an Ecurie. I drew pictures of our surroundings and daily life. Threw in some drawings of fellow soldiers - a few ladies to spice up the days and nights – some cartoon-like commentaries on Fritz, the enemy. I never really showed anyone the sketchpad after I returned, as it didn't seem relative to anything. ~ *I hope my Emma will find it some day and take the trip with me. Share my life. See my thoughts. Understand me better. Maybe look into the archives of McGill University to see what is written about me and the famous Siege Battery 7th. She will not have known me very long as time is even now running out. Too bad. I leave her as a small child, barely eleven, the same age as when I came here to start a new life. I would have liked to have known her as an adult, to see who she might have become. Maybe me in part. I hope so ~*

Enemy bombardment of front lines, the never-ending barrage of those terrible small buggers, aerial torpedoes and rifle grenades.

The constant pounding, thundering sounds of continuous

artillery - the constant ducking as we were confined to clearing trenches and putting up our shelters. The corrugated huts. Those trenches soon to be filled with bodies, some smothered under earth, some simply shot. I draw the scene with clarity and strive for some humour to soften the fear and apprehension and call it Salvo upon Corrugated Iron Hut.
~ *Salvo, funny concept ~ as in a Salute.* SALVO. But here it's the enemy's welcoming salutation of projectiles- aimed at our 'made up' shelters, a simultaneous discharge of artillery. Salvo. Welcome home, Boys. Craters, shrapnel, trenches. Like prairie dogs sitting and waiting. I draw while the phonograph plays out "...for she's ma Rosie" as we settle into our Chateau Beauclaire. Tent homes 'Up The Line', bombs bursting near while fellow friend, Freddy, and I build our 'dig in', only later to dig out fellow comrades fallen and buried under piles of loosened earth, flattening them in a death grip of agony.
~ *I can feel his strong body pressing into mine as we danced around the hut, smell his smell and feel his skin, taste the salt. We were alive. It was simple. WE were alive. I often wonder what happened to my Freddy?* ~ I remember reading a journal by Frederick Palmer – *My Second Year of the War*. He had stated it so very clearly and simply.

"*Bundles of rocket flares, empty ammunition boxes, steel helmets crushed in by shell-fragments, gasbags, eye-protectors against lachrymatory shells, spades, water bottles, unused rifle grenades, egg bombs, long stick-handled German bombs, map cases, bits of German "K.K." bread, rifles, the steel jackets of shells and unexploded shells of all calibers were scattered about the field between the irregular welts of chalky soil where shell fire had threshed them to bits ... they talked shop about the latest wrinkles in fighting; how best to avoid having men buried by shell-bursts; the value of gas and lachrymatory shells; the ratio of high explosives to shrapnel; methods of "cleaning out" dugouts or "doing in" machine guns, all in a routine that had become an accepted part of life like the details of the stock carried and methods of selling in a department store.*" ~ And for me, Eric James, I had spent two years of my life in that hellhole and I want to shout out now. Here and now. But to no avail and for no purpose. The snow cushions my mouth, my thoughts.

    I would serve two different tours of duty, one on ground and one in the air.

And then a terrible day – my first visit to No.1 CGH Etaples - the field hospital. The area around Etaples is teaming with great concentrations of Commonwealth reinforcement camps and hospitals. We are the *Storm Troopers* as Fritz calls us after we took Vimy Ridge, a vantage point thought impossible after several attempts by the Brits and French ~ Canada, Australia, New Zealand, South Africa, India, all part of this group and almost instantly recognized as THE rising superpower for its soldiers' bravery and tactics. Us. They were all talking about us.

Etaples was remote enough from attack, except from aircraft, and railway accessible from both the northern and / or southern battlefields. Imagine, just imagine, in 1917, 100,000 troops camped among the sand dunes and the hospitals, included are eleven general, one stationary, and four Red Cross hospitals and a convalescent depot.

It was quite a sight. 22,000 wounded or sick could be dealt with here. There. And then No. 5 Etaples. ~ *This was the War to end all wars. THE GREAT WAR FOR CIVILIZATION. That's what my medal is inscribed with.* We Allied Powers - Serbia, Russia, France, Britain, Belgium, Romania, Italy, etc.. and the Americans only entering in 1917 after that German U-boat sank a boat loaded with civilians vs. The Central Powers of Germany, Austria-Hungary, the Ottoman Empire (the horsemen of the day) and Bulgaria. ~ *I wonder if the U-boat hadn't sunk those civilians would they have entered?* ~

In September 1919, ten months after the Armistice, three hospitals and the Q.M.A.A.C. convalescent depot remained. ~ *Time blurs from one day to another. One year to another. One period to another. Interchangeable. Pages of my life. Past. Present. No future. Here. Seemingly trapped in this reel.*

I caption the picture day "Surprise somebody really cares whether you were alive or not" as I will draw pictures of the nurses and hospital staff. 101.5 temperature, a 'cough' and 'breathe please'. I watch bodies being taken away for transfer and / or burial. ~ *Always try for a little humour in the sketches. Got to keep one's sanity and measure of humanity alive.*

I return for a short time to Montreal. No worse for wear, as I have all limbs and sight, minus my lovely head of once auburn hair. The war is still ongoing. I enter McGill and start an academic life in Civil Engineering. 1916. Meet up with Ross Hutchison who will

become a steadfast friend throughout my life. A good Scotsman with similar values and interests. We will be aldermen together at the Anglican Church – the breakaway reformed Henry VIII church. Ross had a keen sense of humour and an eye for business.
And again, I reenter the battlefield. My life is once again disrupted. It is 1917 and I am twenty-one. This time, as part of a regiment of fellow students - the McGill Battery Siege, first known as the 6th then became the 7th, Canadian Garrison Artillery.
Ross is part of the group. I was promoted to Acting Sergeant before my transfer to RAF. Anzin is located in the Nord, Nord Pas de Calais region of France, once the centre of important coal mines situatedin the Valenciennes basin and belonging to the Anzin Company with its formation dating back to 1717. Hence, Anzin. The metallurgical industry of the place is so extensive - iron and copper foundings and the manufacture of steam engines, machinery, a varietal of heavy iron goods and chain-cables. Maybe those are the reasons for the interest – Fritz' passion. Back in the trenches for another shell stint (TEAR). Gas shells (TEAR) – lachrymatory agents, from the Latin tear. Basically a non-lethal chemical weapon that stimulates the corneal nerves in the eyes causing tears, pain and sometimes blindness. ~ *Don't believe what you read. It kills the brain, the eyes, the skin, the spirit* ~ '*Don't rub your eyes. Let them tear.*' *My God that was painful. I can feel that heat, the sting, and the pain. It feels like now, then, as I lie on the snow. The searing. But the smell isn't here. That putrid smell of rotting. At F. A. in Anzin in a can shed for three days.* ~ *I have fallen down a hellhole of reliving. Bad timing. Bad thoughts. Stuck in the mud. Stuck, can't shake the past, yet* ~
Military trucks and horse drawn wagons of artillery and supplies – Abele-Poperinghe Road to and from the battlegrounds of Ypres. Those warhorses were initially essential to the offensive elements of the military force – the military cavalry and cavalry charges. But over time, their vulnerability to machine guns and artillery fire soon reduced their utilitarian use. Tanks replaced them and became the dominant ground force, then air followed. Hundreds of thousands of horses died and oh so many more were treated in veterinary hospital only to be sent back to the front. Equine food was a major issue. The Germans lost many due to starvation.

Nine Elms, a name given by the Army to a group of trees. Yes trees. 460 meters east of the Arras-Lens main road, between Thelus and Roclincourt. That is also where the cemetery was begun, after the capture of Vimy Ridge – the 14th Canadian infantry Battalion who fell on April 9, 1917. *~ Bethune, Bruay-la-Buissiere, Amiens. All memorable cities then and when revisited with my Charlotte. Sweet Charlotte. Bold Charlotte.*

Days at CCS at Aubigny a village approximately 15 klm northwest of Arras on the road to St. Po. Casualty Clearing Station. I needed to get off the ground and get into the air. I transferred to the RAF. Started at Folkestone. From there to Hastings then to Durham – Aeroplanes were just coming into military use when the war started, reconnaissance mostly. We engineers and pilots learned from experience – what worked and what didn't. It was learn on the job. And learn quickly. I was assigned to Folkestone, which was one of the main embarkation points for troops heading for the Western Front. Many of the larger houses in the town were being used as rest camps for us soldiers from the battlefields. At Shorncliffe Military Camp thousands of men were camped, including a large contingent of us from Canada. The main line of communication from the Western Front to London ran through the town. My transfer put me in as second in command of the Squadron with King George VI, better known as Captain Windsor. A smart, clever man who liked people and they liked him. He was a man's man. A *people* man. *~ Flight A. Squadron D. An interesting time.*

I had been stationed out of Folkestone in time to experience the infamous raid that took place 25th May 1917 – an enemy plane circled over the town around Tontine Street. All the inhabitants were unaware of what was to happen as most thought it an exercise or one of *ours* from Dover. The approach was from the west. There was another attack at Hythe and Shorncliffe Camp, at the west end of Folkestone itself around Central Station and Bouverie Road East. I remember reading about the exact moment from eyewitness reports as I was *readying* in the squad room. That was the last time we sat unprepared, without alert signals. The cemetery and the famed Royal Victoria Hospital mortuaries were soon filled and even the West Cliffe and Shornclife military hospitals were used for the inured. The Canadian Army Medical Corps and Special Police were brought in to help with the removal of the dead and injured. This attack on unprotected and unprepared civilians shook the nation. It was the falling from the sky – dropping bombs on civilians, that was the clincher. It was a terrorist act again innocent persons. The visual of torn limbs and smouldering flesh. ~ I need to leave the war theme now. To lie in wait and move on with my ever fleeting present to a happier time. To a productive time. To a living time. I have not spent this much energy on thoughts of war since I was that young man in the thick of it all. I leave my present for a respite to feel something. Anything. The cold white, I drift to the chalk building. But I am stuck in the time period. Not released, yet.

    Marsh Court, built by Lutyens, Sir Edwin Lutyens, in 1901, taking until 1904 to complete, for friend, Huber Johnston, sportsman, adventurer, and stockbroker. I enjoyed my brief encounter with him never realizing that I might again meet him under totally different circumstances. When I returned as an emissary. But enough, until later. Built of chalk, white chalk, gleaming local white chalk. Turned into a hospital for recovering soldier by the owners during the war, I was sent there after an explosion to convalesce for several months. Marsh Court was perched high above one of Britain's most exclusive fishing rivers, The Test, and surrounded by incredible gardens designed by Gertrude Jekyll. Sunken gardens and the pergola, the arbor forming a shaded walkway, the passageway to yet another life complete with its adjacent stone pools and sweeping lawns – the many terraces taking advantage of the natural fall of the ground. Formal elements of gardens and mazes, stone walks, bird pools. An incredible place in which to recover. *~ And I'm sure that my continued interest in water, the bubbling, rushing waters, teeming with fish and gardens, lovely gardens that stretch endlessly onward, was permanently etched into my memory, like a fine pen nib tracing across a sheer blank piece of paper. Those solitary walks through the endless lawns, the wading knee high in waters rushing over rocks and I casting a line into the clear waters in hopes of a trout. My life is the line and I have cast deep into the waters, the rushing waters and have found my trout, time and time again. I sigh. It took so much out of my life, this time, this war. That war. There are times when I can not flee it. It hangs and devours my soul. My spirit. My mind. And yet ~*

    I am a TTF. Time Traveling Functionary. I am that agent

ambassador, envoy, go-between, promoter, servant, steward, surrogate. I move between different points in time analogous to moving between different points in space. It is all interconnected and without seam. My purpose is to learn and understand the planet and its inhabitants. To share ideas and live as one for the time period allotted by the very life span I've taken on – to experience every thing as it would be, even to die, and then to be suspended in energy until a new host is found, transmitting the information through experience to a home base housing information, solely. One very large brain-cell, as it were, that encompasses all from the Beginning to the End in one endless ripple. Seamless.

*I AM as a lucid dream, from which I move through interspecies. I AM of esoteric energies, a type of élan vital, differentiating me from non-living objects, the **q**i in Taoist philosophy, **prana** in Hindu belief ~ **etheric**, a name given by neo-Theosophy to that vital body - the first layer in the human energy field, yet to be, yearning to be in immediate contact with that physical body, but always, yes always, sustaining and connecting it with the higher bodies. All interesting theories bandied about since the beginning of time by philosophers and religious figures from Madame Blavatsky to Besant, and interestingly by Dr. Walter J. Kilner who gained his popularity after the war in 1914-1918. My war. He talked a great deal about the layer of the 'human atmosphere rendering visibility' to the naked eye through certain exercise. Just think of all those grieving wives and lovers, friends and family members yearning to learn the resolving exercise. To connect and be connected with. Clearly the good doctor must have tapped into those war ghosts lost in man's furtive display of inhumanity to himself.*

*You might well ask how it is that I can become part of the very fabric of time and space. Actually **become** it. As with my mother Lily who had given birth to me. In a sense she had. Her birth child clung to the brink of mortality, due to some complication that ought not to have happened. I simply took hold of the situation and became that child with all its birth rights, good and bad, and made our life, my life rich in experience, in the need or ought I say, the mission to educate and be educated, to share what knowledge I might garnish while in this temporal structure, to share my pleasures, hopes and fears, and possibly shape ideas for the next generation of mortals to* *come. Not a shape shifter but a true energy that roots, nourishes and is nourished and then experiences 'en totale' the meaning of life.*

I am the Linga Sharira, the invisible double of the human body, the doppelganger, bioplasmic body, the matrix. That classical element of Platonic and Asistoleoan physics which continued into my Victorian times. Alice Bailey, born in Manchester a few years before me, became a fond friend in later life. I did so enjoy her thoughts on this very subject. She was not far off the truth. She and her A. A. Materials as her followers were to call them, her words, her works. She was a believer that the Masters of the Ancient Wisdom, as she would call them, were a brotherhood of enlightened, all working under the guidance of he who called himself Maitreya. The name Maitreya (Metteyya in Pāli) is derived from the Sanskrit word maitrī (Pāli: mettā) meaning "loving-kindness", which is in turn a derivative of "friend". I am that friend, perhaps. How I love to learn the derivation of words.

Actually Maitreya foretold of a time to come, perhaps, though not yet realized after all these millenniums, when humans become enlightened as to their placement in the universe. An acknowledgement of being one within a whole, rather than the hubris self-notion of being the centre.

As I would say "I have lived a very long time" and indeed I have, for what are fables but stories based on truths? All relative to time and space. From Urashima Taro's first telling in the Nihonig book back in 720 about a young fisherman who visits an undersea palace and stays there for three days, only to find when he returns to his village that he is 300 years into the future. I must admit I was shocked. I laughed then cried. It was a cruel and bitter lesson, which taught me not to become too possessive over the fleeting possessions of life and the body. Maitreya. You were cruel.

Physicist, Dr Nikola Tesla had been quoted: "If you want to find the secrets of the universe, think in terms of energy, frequency and vibration." It must be true as I have soared over the multi-layered jungle canopies, and flown with my geese on their long and arduous transmigrations, fed wild river salmon to my young atop high treetops in remote areas. I have swum with the pods across vast oceans of water, jumped in play with the dolphins; slid the ice banks with the penguins, and sat on my chicks in puffin heaven nestled in bedrock cliffs. I have floated as algae and bobbed along, stretching out my gigantic jell shell as my brethren and I invaded the China coast, heading for the western coast of Japan. We, the lion's mane jellyfish, the ones to be reckoned with.

  I have even allowed small children to dream of riding my back as I, 'master seahorse', floated in the Aquarium tank under dim light. Did you know that I had no eco-skeleton but instead a hard body with bony plates that fused together with a scaleless fleshy covering. So many different shapes and configurations I have undergone. I, seahorse, had survived although less than one in a thousand of us babies, frys as we are called, actually live to adulthood. Predators are everywhere. Life is harsh. Meant only for the strong, and that applies to all living creatures, as far as I have seen throughout my ventures. "I have lived a very long time" Eric James said He is right. We have. He and I.

  Carl Sagan once suggested that (we) time travellers were here and have been here for a long time but were clothed in disguise. Treading perhaps on **closed time** like curves, forming closed loops in spacetime, allowing us return to our own past. Not quite the Time Lord of Dr. Who, which I came to enjoy for its complexities and simplicity, not to mention its political thrust. The truth is true. I return to the cold, fat white snowflakes gently falling over me, covering my existence, and I run with my pack recalling my days in Alaska, circa 1600 as they pass through my veins for a split of a split second. Twelve years, leader, mated and with two cubs of our own.

  We were the Grey Wolf, the largest member of the canidae. Once formidable throughout North America and Eurasia. We are dwindling in number. We were and are still hunted for our pelts, our bones for medical use and for the sheer pleasure of sport hunting. No other creature exhibits this passion. Sport hunting. We are a shy group by nature and difficult to kill having become familiar with the ways of men, their smell, sounds and manner. I taught my clans dogs to dig up the man's traps without tripping them. The hounds were not a match for us but well conditioned horses presented another threat. Now aerial shootings have by far become the most effective way to control us. This was our future. Not so mine. I had moved on already to yet another experience, like the mayfly who lives but one day or the bee three weeks. Such a tactile life, of needs and wits.

I feel the thrill of my life. Past, present and what will be, somewhere, like the days of playing with siblings in the snow in winter and of running the forest bed in fall, chasing butterflies and squirrels and wadding through waters filled with lively fish in spring. Life just keeps going on. As an endless seam, yet seamless. I lie in the snow, those big fat flakes closing in, warming my body. Our body. All relative to time and space.

CHAPTER two ~

I met Charlotte through friends of mine. My first wife, Doris, had died quite unexpectedly crossing the street, hit by a car, and I had been widowed two years now. I was visiting the city, closing up business on a job stationed in Maine when Raoul invited me to dinner. Both he and his wife Souetes, old University chums, in turn asked Charlotte to make the fourth, even though she was recently engaged. Charlotte had declined, naturally, but later did Souetes a favour. It was only for dinner. It was 1929. I had just joined Canada Industries Limited, a nice change from being on the road covering the Eastern Provinces of Canada and occasionally heading into Maine, touching Lynn and Salem, Albany and New York proper. I worked a pulp paper route, being Manager for the Evergreen Company then moved into the insurance end where I was asked to head up inter connectives as liaison with the states. Seven years. I was thirty-four. Charlotte was twenty, and in those days she was considered 'old', the terms were 'spinster' and 'old maid'. She, of course, was none of those. She was exuberant and glamorous. Most of her friends had already married and had children, but Charlotte had not been in a rush. She had *come out* at the Debutante Ball when she was eighteen, not found any of the boys of interest, and had decided to wait for someone who might challenge her. Patrick had been a good choice and he was madly in love with her. They were to be married in five months' time.

The evening was great fun, the food wonderful and eclectic and it was a nice change from *on the road* foods. My house in the suburbs was still under construction as I had bought it for Doris and I was still renovating it from head to foot when she died.

35

Doris, of course, would never see nor set foot in the house. So the speed of work was not crucial any more. It would be finished when it was. I had engineered every aspect of the renovations, having gotten my degree at McGill University in Civil Engineering with a Business minor back in 1922 after the war. That terrible war.

Charlotte was an engaging sort of person, clever and very sexy in a non-sexy kind of way. Hard to explain exactly. The evening was delightful and I thanked Raoul for the invitation. He was always looking out for my interests, it seemed. It wasn't until two weeks later that I got a call from Charlotte asking if I was going to be in town the following weekend. She was giving a party and thought I might enjoy the outing. I accepted and made the necessary preparations. I had been thinking of Charlotte from the moment we met. But, as she was engaged to marry a seemingly nice fellow, Patrick Leach, terrible last name, I obviously didn't think a future could exist, other than maybe as distant friends. Anything else would not have been proper. But to my surprise, when I found myself in the small kitchen tending to the bar orders, I suddenly and without forethought leaned forward and kissed her. She didn't seem to mind though she pulled back and looked at me, stating that she was not available, as I knew. I replied that I did know she was engaged but thought she ought to marry me instead. She smiled then turned to join the party. "I'll keep that in mind." She had replied with that wonderful come-hither smile.

And within three weeks' time we found ourselves standing in front of a magistrate in City Hall, signing marriage papers and exchanging rings. A small civil marriage with friends, Raoul and Souetes, Ross and his wife Katherine, Lily and Ethel, and Jock Thornhill from the new job site. It was a simple ceremony, actually great fun. Nothing formal. We both wore suits. She with a lovely, small, feathered cap. We all headed out to a dinner at the Ritz after and said that when the house was completed we would have a proper party. We did. First Anniversary to be precise.

We took our honeymoon in the Rockies by way of train, then cut down to California, Hollywood and then continued into Montreal via New York. I thought the trip quite exciting. I guess Charlotte would have preferred a European trek – Lake Como, the Amalfi coast.

We did that the following year.

CHAPTER three ~

"There comes a time in every one's life when the extraordinary can manifest itself. Whether it is from a latent hereditary seed or the environment surrounding, the individual has an opportunity to seize that moment and rise above and beyond." That's what they said at my funeral. Odd that I talk about it now, when I am still alive, hanging on, as it were, but then I had been present, as I always am, somewhere.

Change was inevitable. The ride was high after the war simply because we were alive. The decade of rapid expansion in the United States spilled over to Canada, the country to the north. That's how the Americans always talked about us. Still do. That small country to the north. Frankly it gets a bit dry after a while. As if we were not the great nation we already are and will yet become. And then the great crash of '29 happened. The estimated poverty level was a staggering 75% in the United States. Those who had been in the money had cared little for the starving masses. The previous decade had been spent in slashing wages and attempting to break the union, unfortunately with widespread success. Their American Federation of Labor (AFL) had lost a million of its members. Violence was met when faced with a working-class opposition. Detroit police mowed down several thousand demonstrators with machine guns. The South raged a *fear* war with the Gastonia Daily Gazette running "Communism in the south. Kill it!" as their front-page headliner. Leaflets were distributed with anti-labour slogans, "Would you belong to a union which opposes White supremacy?" The National Guardsmen in North Carolina were ordered to shoot to kill unarmed strikers.

Thousand lost their jobs while others were 'asked' to sign loyalty pledges, to lever the union. The tide was beginning to turn. Solidarity would finally win out. The fight back would be hard but it was not to be dissuaded.

Here in Canada, the Toronto Trade and Labour Council which had begun in 1881, soon to be adopted in Montreal, Vancouver, Ottawa and other cities, banded together for the Trades and Labour Congress of Canada handing out rulings on wage disputes, sanitary regulation of workshops, workmen's compensation and the eight-hour day schedule. All this accomplished between 1900 and 1929. The start of the Great Depression and the establishment of the Worker's

Unity League challenged leadership of Canadian labour. By 1935 the unions looked to organize unskilled workers in the industries of the automobile, steel and rubber. The automotive had long been established in Windsor, Ontario by Gordon McGregor who formed the first Ford Motor Co. of Canada, this only a year after Henry, the inventor, had begun his production in Detroit. The Walkerville Wagon Co. Ltd assembled parts and ferried them by wagonload across the Detroit River where soon Canadian Fords were being shipped to the UK. Oshawa, Ontario had become a centre thanks to Colonel McLaughlin, a Canadian pioneer in industry, having converted the thriving family carriage and sleigh business into the soon to be noisy internal combustion engine. The car we know today. And it was then that the Congress of Industrial Organizations, better known as CIO, became a direct challenge to the craft unionism. General Motors in Oshawa joined the United Automobile Workers, a CIO union, adding more than four thousand workers. It was a time of change and of forging alliances, and like the Cold War and rise of anti-Communism in America which led to purging leftists from the union CIO in the states a new creation would be born in 1956 creating the modern Canadian Labour Congress. I was that part. I was that instrument. *~ and here I lie in the snow melting into another existence. Soon but not yet ~*

My company, Canadian Industries Ltd., CIL for short, had been jumpstarted by DuPont. Back in 1877 Lammot DuPont II had yet to merge with Hamilton Powder Company expanding the explosives market. Lammot purchased shares in Hamilton Powder becoming director of the company. Then amalgamating with several smaller companies WWI offered DuPont the opening to serve Canada, its forces and allies with ammunition. He died in 1952 at age 72. We had met on several occasions ~ business and socially.

His predecessor, Lammot DuPont I, born in 1831 in Delaware, graduated from the University of Pennsylvania, patented and invented the inexpensive blasting powder industry using Peruvian and Chilean sodium nitrate. In 1927 the Nobel Plants were reopened with the approach of WWII. The plants had all been closed in 1922 as a secondary markets were not fully realized, then all was torched in huge fire in 1923. The company formed a subsidiary, Defence Industries Limited, employing 4,300 people at its peak with the full company of 33,00. By the war's end the company expanded again taking on entirely new industries and eventually adopting the name of Canadian Industries Limited, reflecting a broader base of activities. CIL grew throughout the depression. An emerging market was a cellophane cellulose film plant outside of Quebec, Shawinigan Falls built in 1932. We have the Swiss chemist Jacques Brandenberger to thank for figuring out *how to* create cloth that repels water. And as we all know, cellophane is made from regenerated *cellulose*, obtained from lignin, plant matter, dissolved in ionic liquids. By 1942 a second nylon plant was built in Kingston, Ontario. Known generically as polyamides these synthetic polymers were first produced on February 28, 1935, by Wallace Carothers at DuPont's research facility at the DuPont Experimental Station. Nylon is one of the most commonly used polymers. And by the advent of WWII all the ladies' legs were smartly covered in nylon. This was the second plant in the world. I repeat, *in the world*. CIL was on the go and I was there, part of it all. Nylon replaced silk, which was scarce during the war. The military applications extended to parachutes and flack vests, and was used in many types of vehicle tires. Machines, screws, gears and components previously cast in metal because of their minimum to low stress components now used nylon. Nylon was the first synthetic thermoplastic polymer to be used successfully commercially. Instrumental to the changes and ties that bind us all. *~ I am there ~*

CHAPTER four~

"Jimmy Kelly's is the spot NOT to be missed" so said Dorothy Kilgallen, the Voice of Broadway / Journal American. "Not for Debutantes." New Yorker chimed in. "Recommended to Diversion Seekers ... still the tops in the Village." Walter Winchel of the Daily Mirror added. "East or West Jimmy Kelly's is my choice by test." Ed Sullivan speaking for the Daily News. And they all were right. It was the place to meet and enjoy. To be seen or not. The year 1935 – wartime was not far away. Yes, another war to end all wars.

Jock Thornhill joined Charlotte and me, Raoul and Souetes Estoya late. He made his apologies but I could see that something was not quite right. He was agitated not by the being late but by something else. I ordered a drink which he bolted down without a moment wasted. Charlotte and Souetes had gone to the powder room and

Raoul was over at the piano requesting some numbers for Souetes. So that left me and Jock.

"You're late Thornhill. Anything wrong?" I asked.

"Nothing I can't set straight." He put the glass down with a clunk.

"Well out with it man. What's the problem?" I asked, picking up his urgency.

"Something not quite right on a liner's ownership. Nothing for you to worry about Eric. I'll handle it in the morning." The junior executive said.

"What ship's ownership are you talking about?"

"Konialitas."

"And how is this affecting us, exactly Thornhill?"

"One of the company's products – slipping away – again, nothing to worry about Eric. I'll handle it in the morning."

"Good to know there Thornhill. Let's not bring the evening down as the ladies are all ready for some fun."

"I suppose that excludes you then." He jabbed back.

"Clever. Weren't you bringing a mate?"

"Coming in later. He'll be here."

"Good. *Evens* are always better." I said as the ladies reappeared, laughing and looking playful.

"I asked Randolph, our piano man, to play some tunes we all like." Raoul said with a smile. "Told him if he didn't we'd join him up there and make asses of ourselves." His smiled broadened. "I'm sure we could accommodate, right Eric?"

"Lampshade." I replied sternly but with humour.

"Now that's funny. And I lived to tell the tale too." Raoul slapped me on the shoulder. "You're a sly bastard."

The Konialitas. News was of an Argentinian, Aris Nassi, who claimed to be part venture in ownership, but who apparently had gone independent. And in what else, I wondered. He had interests in South America as did our ammunition, after all CIL was part and parcel of the Defence Industries, having been born out of the explosives of Hamilton Powder. Europe and the Americas. Mexico included. Nassi had subscripted an old friend Costas Bratnos, in London, to buy up foreign steamships tied up in Rio. Aris Nassi was one very shrewd player, having realized the importance of those tankers. He named his first Arinton, keeping it in Swedish shipyards. He was trying to take up residency in the Big Apple from where he could mange his tankers, his fleet, sailing them under neutral flags ~ Sweden, Panama thus exploiting the high freight rates in the free market, but the FBI had been told to 'hold him up'. But he would not be deterred. He was a clever, clever fellow. He would go very far, I sensed. I would have to meet him and discuss transportation potential.

Thornhill jumped up when he saw his prize. His partner in crime. I watched as a very good looking man entered the arena and then a sinking, no, an exhilarating feeling took over. My head began to swim in pure pleasure. His prize was non other than *my* Freddy Robinson from my days in the metal hut. My dance partner. I had lost contact and had thought nothing more. Time passed and here we all were, now. How extraordinary.

Jock introduced his friend to the group as everyone shook hands and greeted him into the fold, as it were. "So fellow mates, this is my friend Ronnie Gently. Not a bad catch, eh?" Jock smiled widely with pride. Raoul and Souetes reached forward and welcomed the new man in. Charlotte did the same with a sly smile and a slight nod to Jock.

"Nice to finally meet the mystery man." I said as I shook his hand, possibly holding it a bit longer than I ought to have.

"Likewise." Ronnie answered as he looked hard at me then moved his eyes to include everyone.

"What was that all about?" Charlotte asked.

"What was what?" I answered.

"Do you know him from somewhere?"

"Thought I did but obviously not." I replied.

"He seems a nice fellow, certainly good looking and Jock is in heaven." She smiled.

"Yes he is." I answered with an inner smile. "They both are."

How life keeps one on the *whirl*. Never quite what it appears. Always interesting.

"So what line of business are you in Ronnie?" Raoul asked as he ordered a drink from the girl who had been summoned over by Jock.

"He's a trust fund baby." Thornhill jumped in with enthusiasm. Almost proud of the information.

"Sounds expensive." Charlotte said smiling. "But what exactly do you do?"

"Spy." He answered curtly. "I'll have a Scotch neat please."

Charlotte burst out laughing then tried to compose herself enough to further the question started by Raoul.

"Spy. That covers a lot of ground I should think. Care to focus it a little there, Mr. Gently?"

"Industrial." He replied then looked over at me for a moment and smiled. "Your wife took me literally I think Mr. James." He smiled.

"Eric. Call me Eric. And yes, with the way you presented yourself, I would be inclined to go along with her thinking. So Industrial Espionage. Sounds very hush hush." took Charlotte's hand. "Is it and are you?" I responded as I gave my drink order to the cocktail waitress. "Also a Scotch neat please and a Tequila Sunrise for my wife." Charlotte smiled. "We are very friendly with Mexico, as of late. Both in trade tourism and business. Charlotte grew to love the taste. Interesting plant. Always looking at the plants we are."

"Yes the plants." Ronnie replied. I knew my Freddy was home and wondered if Thornhill was aware of anything or simply too smitten to realize what and who he had here.

"Another time for business. This is a break-away night and the ladies are looking to dance and enjoy themselves so we men will simply have to curb ourselves – no shop talk." I rose and took my Charlotte's hand and escorted her to the dance floor. Raoul followed with Souetes. We loved to 'take to the floor' as we four often chose to dine out and dance the night away. Something about moving to the music, dipping now and then, feeling the hot breath on the neck and taking in the smell of the skin mixed with perfume. Sexy and excitingly reassuring.

From time to time I glanced over my shoulder to watch the two of them chatting and sharing humour together. An interesting couple. Gentry a good ten years older than the junior associate. Freddy hadn't changed much – had lost some of his red hair, though still had more than I had. Walked with a slight limp. Not sure if that was for real or part of the role. Not sure what the role was. Would have to find out.

** ** ** ** **

I met Raoul when I returned from the War, the second time. He was a good looking, well built, short man with a head of hair that was the envy of most men, certainly me. He loved clothes and enjoyed a good time. We were a good fit. He had moved into the room next to mine on campus. His major was International Finance with intent to import and export everything from wines, foods, and diamonds. His cousin, Avila Velazquez, lived in Amsterdam. Cousin Velazquez had worked the South African diamond mines as a mining engineer with Ernest Oppenheimer, the German who immigrated to Britain. Ernest had founded the mining giant Anglo American with J.P. Morgan, the American financier in 1927, taking over DeBeers, a company originally founded by Cecil Rhodes, financed by Alfred Beit and Rothchild. To say Raoul was connected was an understatement.
~ *I met Ernest while doing business in London and we struck up an interesting relationship. Born fifteen years before me he died last year in 1957.* ~

Raoul's uncle was a big-wig in the government, the Mexican government. Little did I realize that he would in fact become the next President. At the time, his uncle was a relatively little known career military officer. But 1940 was hovering around the corner and with it his election. A Roman Catholic and a believer, contrasted against the former anticlerical positions of most since the Revolution, he was slow to enforce the more populist articles of the constitution. Land reform was slow in moving and he promoted private ownership. His conservative bent was also felt in the labour movement, especially when dealings with the rights of strikers. Labour leaders were replaced and within a few years there would be an alienation causing lost textile and building industry workers. A time ripe for 'funny business' as Charlotte would call it ~ anything that smelled of conspiracy or espionage.

And when two tankers were sunk by German submarines, Mexico, who had attempted to remain neutral after the United States had entered the war in '41, was forced to declare war on Germany, which in turn forced the creation of a national security policy to be initiated to counter Axis espionage against Mexico, defending Mexican oil fields and military industries. Mexico's participation in the war effort was one of supply, both labour and raw materials, to the United States. That is not to diminish their losses in the Pacific theatre by their fighter squadron. And so Raoul was brought into the *game* by his uncle who needed information for and against. His enlistment, even though several years before the war, allowed things and events to fall into place, as for example the meeting at the National Palace which became the perfect screen as the meeting itself would be seen as a declaration of solidarity in face of a war.

I liked Raoul. He was quick minded, imaginative, fun to be with and someone who understood life and the fact that we were part of history ~ history in the making. He married Souetes shortly after they met at a campus dance and following in our footsteps, they married within three months' time. Opposite to ours though, there's was a very big wedding followed by an even larger 'after' party. Souetes was an excellent buffer for him. She kept him grounded and sparked. She was a spitfire with a brain to match. A glamour woman, never a girl, born woman for sure. She wore her hair long and lush and she, too, loved clothes and a good time. When we all met she was completing her masters in quantum physics. She spoke German fluently and carried both a Canadian and Brazilian passport. She was multi faceted to many, as I would find.

The Estoya family was connected financially to some of the best families in Europe. Maybe that was why Raoul accepted Estoya as *his* name or as he often said, "Souetes' name sounds better with my name – Raoul Estoya, better than Raoul Camancho." Actually he was right. It did have a better ring to it. And why not? In Montreal the woman always retains her name in business and on documents. I reminded Charlotte that if she were ever to enter a hospital I would have to track her down with her maiden name and thank goodness she had a good sounding one. Bales. Charlotte Bales.

How we all became connected is a wonder, as I had neither connections, money nor any particular flavour to offer. But apparently I had something to offer, aside from my good Yorkshire humour and stunning looks. The three of us thrived together and when Charlotte joined it was a merry foursome. We travelled to Mexico on a regular basis. I loved the climate and the food – warm and spicy. Charlotte loved it because of the flowers and the art. "Just look at those flowers, Eric; their size and colour. And the art is so vibrant and earthy. Rich in sensuality." I could hear her voice overflowing with enthusiasm as she would plan her days with Souetes. Raoul and I did our business. I never talked about it and she never asked. And every now and then Souetes would join Raoul giving Charlotte and I our time off on our own. Our every need was always first class. Provided by Raoul's uncle, I thought, though Raoul always claimed that Souetes' parents liked to lavish her in ways she herself never would. Neither of us had any children at this point in time so we enjoyed our singularity away from parenthood.

CHAPTER five ~

"Ronnie? Suits you quite." I said as I put my hat down on the table. Ronnie had taken a small out of the way room in old town near the docks. He and Thornhill lived in a rather swank apartment off Sherbroooke Street near Cedar. Two mates living together was not thought odd nor suspicious, just thrifty. Their relationship went unchallenged. They were *men about town*, always in the company of women, good-looking women. Men on the rise in the business world.

"Thanks. I've often thought about you. Wondered what had happened. Heard you were at The Marsh for recovery for awhile before being shipped back, where ever that was." Freddy seemed a bit nervous or possibly not sure of his posture, his feelings.

"That's right. Had a second tour as well, serving with Captain Windsor. Was his *second* actually. Nice chap. Enjoyed his humour. Seemed to *get* the common touch. Enjoying life now with Charlotte."

I looked out the window and smiled. I was remembering how I used to spend my time here. By the docks It was like coming home in an odd way. "And how are things with Jock Thornhill? When did that start up or ought I to ask how?"

"Just one of those things, Eric. It just happened and then it kept on and then we were. Comfortable. He's a tad young and thinks all things will resolve themselves in the best of ways." He laughed a bit too easily as he passed the drink. "Scotch, Neat."

"Thanks. I can do with one. Long day and getting longer." I smiled. "So a trust fund baby. That's the ruse, is it?"

"Seems that a high end play-boy is more exciting than the truth and what with the way the world is playing itself out, why not."

"And will they resolve themselves in the best of ways? The issues of the world?" I said taking a sip. I licked my lips. "Nice."

"Doubt that. Seems we are headed for a second war to end all wars. I've come to the conclusion that we humans like to thin out the herd from time to time, wreak havoc on lives and dreams and then after the dust settles, we simply start again, preparing for the next. There is always a next, somewhere."

"Somewhat fatalistic, aren't you Ronnie?" I took a sip. "I should call you Ronnie so as not to loose the thread."

"Yes on both answers. Who wouldn't be after the metal huts, *tears* and salvo. I mean really. Rose still playing her tune?" He paced back and forth for a moment. He was getting restless.

"Yes and no, Ronnie. Yes and no." I answered with a metered voice. So much water had passed under the bridge I wondered why I was there. What was I thinking when I accepted his invite.

"So would I call you a Humint person?"

"I see you're current Eric. Yes. I fall into that category of intelligence gathered from information provided by human sources, human intelligence. Interrogations and conversations with those who I think will give me access to information." He paused. "I think that about covers it as the manual might have said." Ronnie smiled then paced a bit.

"And was Thornhill one of those interrogations and/or conversations. Did he give you access, Ronnie?"

"Yes."

"And do you think I am or will?"

"No. That's not why you're here."

"Then why am I here, Ronnie?"

"Because I've missed you. Because when I saw you I knew you *saw* me. That's why you're here. Am I not right, Eric?"

I paused for a moment. This would be a turning point I thought. The answer would lead me down a path and into something that I might not like or want to go to, at this point in my life, or it might prove very good on many fronts. A turning point. A choice had to be made. I had to make it.

"You were a sight for sore eyes, Freddie. Indeed you were. And here we are." I answered as I took off my suspenders and unbelted my pants. I kicked off my shoes and dropped my drawers like a burlesque girl no longer in training. A funny sight. Tie and shirt still on but naked where it counted. Interesting. Life moves in mysterious ways.

"Glad you're up for it Eric." Ronnie smiled. His hand cupped the erect white elephant in the room and we both laughed. "Nice to have you back." Ronnie said as he unzipped his pants and let them fall to the floor. "Shall we dance?"

**** ******* ******

"Raoul and Souetes asked us over for drinks tomorrow, if that's alright?" Charlotte asked as she combed out her hair in front of the vanity in the bedroom. "Is that alright, Eric?" She stroked methodically.

"Yes. Yes that's alright, Charlotte. Fine." I answered as I came out of the shower, grabbing a towel and taking up the bathrobe hanging on the door back. "Any particular reason or just …?"

"Because, and why not I suppose." Charlotte answered quietly, then continued. "You were with Ronnie, weren't you?"

"Yes. Yes I was. He called at the office and asked me over for a drink. It appears we had met before."

"In the metal hut."

"Yes, in the metal hut. In another time and place. I had thought he had – actually I don't know what I thought. We just fell out of contact and time passed and here I am with you and then he walked in with Thornhill. Quite a surprise." I paused.

"I imagine it was. And I take it you don't want Thornhill or anyone else to know that you knew him once. Is that right?"

"Yes, for now. He said he was recruited after I left the field."

"By whom?"

"Wouldn't say."

"For what?"

"Wouldn't say."

"Then why tell you?"

"Said I was different and that I understood."

"And do you?"

"Yes. He's a Humint. On assignment I believe."

"Is Thornhill his assignment?"

"Don't think so. I just think that happened. But he runs in interesting circles and some that might be of use to us." I pulled back the bed covers and took off my robe. "Come to bed, Charlotte. It's late."

"And did you and Ronnie go to bed?"

"Yes. Yes we did. Are you offended or horrified?"

"Neither Eric. Not quite sure what to think. I know you love me and I you. I suppose the thought of you with a man is intriguing in an odd way, again not sure how or why." She put the brush down neatly and straightened the area. "We are being extremely civilized, aren't we, having this talk the way we are?" She laughed. "Oh what my mother would say? Divorce the man or don't ask questions and simply be." Charlotte came over to the bed and sat down. "But that's not the way we are, is it? I mean we talk things out even if they are a bit weird."

"Are they weird?" I asked taking her nightgown gently off her shoulders. "Am I?"

"Well if you aren't then I certainly must be." She turned around and looked me in the eye. "But it seems to work for us so I guess that's the answer."

She kissed me hard on the lips running her tongue over the outside, back and forth, back and forth. I loved her foreplay as it only kindled more feelings. "So nice to have you Charlotte. Thank you." I said quietly as I embraced her into my body, as I slowly blanketed her underneath me, her smells curling into my nostrils making my body rise gently and constantly. I reached over and turned off the bed light.

CHAPTER six ~

Charlotte had joined my mother at the Decarie fields and in the kitchen, on and off for some time now, during the weekdays. My Charlotte thought helping out and learning the farming business with Mrs. Decarie and husband, Anatole, might just be the ticket, besides it gave her time to talk things out with Lily, as both women were from very different backgrounds, with me being the common link.

Charlotte's mother was a society woman who had married into her position. Her mother's mother, Louise, had actually come from Brittany and had settled on Ile Orleans where they farmed the land. Not as lowly farmers but as landowners and investors. They had come from money but it had all but been used up, wisely and not so. Charlotte's mother, Grace, did not really like my mother as she felt her beneath her. She was civil but that was about it. Charlotte's relationship with Lily was the bane of Grace's existence but she was wise enough not to intrude. She simply did not have to associate. And she didn't. And that extended to me, I might add. Grace's husband, Frank, kept a closer eye on my career as he felt it reflected on him and as he was no longer *in the game* I was *the player* to watch. I didn't mind any of this. It was what it was and that was that.

"Good to see you today, Lily," Charlotte cheerfully said as she embraced the older woman with fondness. "I have been thinking about the garden and what Eric and I might be planting this season. He talked about raising chickens and I'm all for it. I think it a great idea." Charlotte took her place in the kitchen next to Lily who was working on filling the jam jars and getting all ready for the next shipment. Mrs. Decarie had put Lily in charge of most of the operation as she had found my mother a very able mind.

"How many were you contemplating?" Lily asked with interest.

"That was what I thought you might advise us on. Maybe six or eight, enough to give eggs but not too many to be too much of a bother. Eric is making a very exciting hen house with a dormer for laying and a sliding shelf to gather the eggs. There will be a free sliding exit for them complete with sliding shelves, giving way to the floors for clean out of the coop itself. We were thinking of letting them run free during the day on the back part of the property as there are plenty of grubs and other things. Cut down on the chicken feed itself." Charlotte was excited about the new project. Deep down, aside from the glamour and the society needs, she was a farm girl, of sorts. She liked the smell of new mowed hay, the smell of horses and cows ~ "Nature's perfume" she would say. I simply thought it pungent.

"My that is elaborate isn't it?" Lily responded as she capped the jars she had finished filling in the jam kitchen.

"Well you know how Eric likes to do things. Loves to build and give a great presentation." Charlotte packed the jars into a box at the side. "He's so clever, really." She continued, "so very clever." Charlotte turned to Lily and asked, "Was he always this way? I mean, thorough?"

"Yes and no."

"Now you sound like Eric." Charlotte laughed. "Just like him."

"He obviously learned from the best." Lily joined in the laughter then continued. "He was always the odd one. I think from was born there had been some kind of complication? Never quite understood the problem. That child clung to life hovering on the brink of his very end and then, as if given a breath, a new breath of life, he regenerated himself into a healthy child."

"Regenerated?" Charlotte broke in.

"Yes. I do believe regenerated is the proper word." Lily thought for a moment recalling the happening. "Always clever and mindful. Always sassy and fun loving. Someone who relished life, even under the harshest of conditions." Lily resumed her lidding in silence as if thinking out their past together. "He had a terrible time in the war. It took so much out of him, as it did for everyone who was there too, of course. Ethel, his sister, never talks about the actual war, only of the people she met and how interesting they were. From all walks of life and she's maintained friendships with many of them from all over the world. And she visits them from time to time, they knowing how to incorporate their needs to see her so that the University can live with or rather, live with her gallivanting all over the world. They say it's for business. Now she's quite the woman." Lily closed off with great pride. "I guess I like my children."

Charlotte picked up the conversation. "So how many birds do you think?"

"I'd go with eight. You've got enough space for them and they won't be too much trouble. Just talk to them to get them back home at night. You want them to know that they live somewhere and that *that* place is egg laying home otherwise you'll be looking all over for the eggs. Are you planning on selling them?"

"Yes. I thought we could do eggs, some of our garden foods, and the cherries when they're in season. I've already spoken with Jean Talon who heads up a local farmer market and he's fine with us joining the others. Almost everyone is French and actual growers for a living, but he's open minded enough to know our presence might bring in some buyers who might not otherwise come in. Not to sound snooty but you know what I mean. We being Anglophones."

She laughed heartily. "Et dire que nous n'avons pas progressé très loin pendant toutes ces années. Eh bien peut-être que c'est un peu dur. Nous sommes le mélange un peu mieux. Peut-être. Or ought I to say and to think we haven't progressed very far in all these years. Well maybe that's a bit harsh. We are blending a bit better. Perhaps."

"It's so good to hear you speak such nice French, Charlotte.

I've always taught my children that languages can break or make friendships and why not expand one's horizons through word."

"You certainly taught Eric well. He's prolific in several now. He added Spanish last year and he has been thinking of taking up Japanese. Says 'the times they are a changing and we need to expand across the seas more.' "

"Does he now?" Lily muttered.

Lilly died in the summer of 1940. The same year I joined the Freemasonry. She just didn't wake up one morning. If there had been anything wrong I didn't know and she hadn't said. I think she simply thought she had *spent her time* and that it had been enough. It was that simple. She was that kind of woman.

We had not had any children, which was too bad, because she would have loved to have been a grandmother. It seems her children weren't very good producers. Ethel was of a different persuasion and Jack and Rena had no interest other than in each other. I decided then and there that if Charlotte and I could not conceive ourselves we would adopt. We did seven years later and called her Emma, after Lily's mother. Lily was buried with a simple funeral. Mrs. Decarie and Anatole, now both very, very old, offered to supply the food for the *wake*. Anatole acknowledged Lily with a plaque he placed on the fence by the vegetable garden where they worked along side each other. The kitchen also hung up her favourite apron *in retirement*. It was all very touching.

A simple woman who had made such an impact on so many for being herself. She was young. She was seventy.

I would miss my mother as she had been my sounding board throughout the many years. And I would come to miss our dinners in the garden. She had left a silver bracelet embedded with some gemstones to Charlotte. Lily had never said just where she had acquired it but it was very special to her and it was good to see Charlotte wearing it in both appreciation of the woman who had given it to her and because it was truly a special piece.

CHAPTER seven ~

Canada was experiencing an exciting and somewhat turbulent time. It was 1930 and the child was feeling growing pains. ~ *I lived the history. Took part in the history. Made the history* ~ It started with the federal election in which Richard Bennett became prime minister. He initiated an aid package of $20million for the unemployed during the depression and strengthened Canada's trade by initiating preferential tariffs although the export markets continued to fall. It was the same year that Ethel's friend, Cairine Wilson became the first female Senator in Canada. Quite a coup. In 1931 we saw the Balfour Report of 1926 being finally authorized thus allowing the Governor General to take the status of official representative of the Crown, only to relinquish that power when the reigning monarch touched Canadian soil. We were moving away from the *Mother* head, in spirit.

    1932 sadly saw the Relief Camps take root, military in nature, in an attempt to cope with the single man unemployed during the depression. Robert Bennett proposed that the men be paid 20cents a day in return for a 44-hour week of hard labour. They were housed in bunkhouses. It was not popular but served for a time. But presence of these camps would ultimately lead to the ON-TO-OTTAWA trek taking place June 3 to July 1, 1935 where over one thousand unemployed men from all over the western provinces marched, en mass, to Ottawa to confront PM Bennett regarding the atrocities occurring at the camps. This was the beginning of Bennett's downfall as PM.

    The Ottawa Agreement set a stage for preferential trade between other Commonwealth nations and Canada. Canada had stepped directly into the ranks of high tariff countries. The Customs Act was amended, giving the government broad reaching arbitrary valuations power to impose what effectively was prohibitive duties on imports from countries with depreciated currencies. The Ottawa Conference. ~ *I was there as an advisor* ~ The importation of lumber, coal, asbestos and several other products from Russia was prohibited. And in retaliation the Soviet government ceased purchasing from Canada. Trade was resumed in 1936 a year after the tariff war with Japan occurred. They viewed this 'administrative position' as nothing short of discriminatory practices. Negotiations failed to resolve the issue so Japan imposed a surtax of 50 cents which was countered by Canada's surtax of 33 1/3 cent on all goods. An amicable settlement was effected five months later. Since Canada had opened its Tokyo legation, the first in Asia, and Japan its consulate legation in Ottawa back in 1929, open dialogue had been ongoing.

A Legation is differentiated from an Embassy in that it is made up of an Envoy Extraordinary, a Minister Plenipotentiary (of second class rank somewhere between a Minister Resident / Ambassador but with full powers to represent the government). *~ I smile thinking of how I reminded Charlotte that getting a new language skill would come in handy ~* So the Imperial Economic Conference was held in Ottawa in 1932. And it was here that a comprehensive series of bilateral agreements were signed by the United Kingdom (Britain), The Irish Free State, Southern Rhodesia and South Africa. Australia and New Zealand had already signed the pact. Canada had no special agreement with India. *~ I might be told, if it were possible, that at my funeral dignitaries from Japan flew in to pay homage to the man from Yorkshire who on many occasion had acted as go-between and friend in tight places around the negotiating tables. Theirs was a land I grew to love. And the many Asian influences I came away with from my travels on behalf of trade relations were evident in our home. The large white house, as it was called. ~*

Mass communication for the masses. The formation of the CBC, Canadian Broadcasting Corporation, radio, was forged and the creation of the Bank of Canada followed in 1934.

The Union Nationale was established in 1935 when Conservative Maurice Duplessis allied with the Liberals under Paul Gouin, a splinter group, in order to remove the then corrupt Liberal Administration, causing the re-election of Liberal Mackenzie King as PM, a position he would hold throughout World War II (1939-1945).

And then in 1936 Gouin was ousted from the Union by his former ally Maurice Duplessis who became Premier of Quebec. *~ Duplessis would later present me with the keys to my own city, the city of Montreal, for service to my community of fellow Canadians – my country - always there, in the now. Oh how proud my mother would have been. Charlotte certainly was ~*

The Rowell-Sirois Commission came into existence in 1937 in order to investigate financial relationship between provincial government and federal. Canadians realized that living in a country with considerable regional disparities required a new way of governing. The modern world was now: radio and mass circulating newspapers, plane travel highlighted by Trans Canada Air Lines which began its regular flight schedules, the increase use of railways – these medias put Canadians more in contact with one another than before developing a sense of common identity. Those citizens in poorer regions found it difficult to accept lesser social services, perhaps even inferior quality, than those in richer provinces. The have-not provincial governments could achieve equality only by imposing heavier than average financial burdens on their own taxpayers. These disparities had become unacceptable. Government action intervention was the answer regarding health insurance but many of the other suggestions were sacked only to be revisited in a post war society.

And then for the first time ever, an American President made an official visit to Canada. 1938. A meeting was held with Canadian Prime Minister Mackenzie King in Kingston, Ontario, attended by top financial managers. *~ I was there ~ and so the stage of history was being explored.*

CHAPTER eight ~

I met Aris, quite by chance, while out on the town at Billy Rose's Diamond Horseshoe, Paramount Hotel, New York. He had taken quite a fancy to my Charlotte who I must admit looked truly spectacular that evening. Not that she didn't always but there was a glow in her very presence that evening. He sent a tall bottle of vintage champagne over to the table and then raised his glass in salute. Raoul and Souetes were charmed by his gesture and delighted at the attention given us as Aris had become quite the man in the Big Apple. Ronnie and Thornhill had come along for the evening as had Ross and Katherine. We were a merry group, to be sure.

"Shall we invite him over to share?" Charlotte asked with a smile.

"I think that would be appropriate." I replied. "Waiter," I signalled. "Please send our appreciation for the bottle and invite the gentleman to join us, if you would."

The dashing young man smiled and put down his napkin and followed the waiter to our table, where another chair was promptly added, complete with place setting.

"Thank you for the invitation to join your party." He said with ever the slightest of accents. Sounded more Greek than South American, I thought.

"Our pleasure that you accepted and in turn, thank you for the wonderful bottle. A nice way to break the ice." I replied.

Thornhill jumped in "Aris Nassi, the tanker king?" He asked as if this man was 'new' to him, a hard fact since Aris was in all the papers as of late. But for Ronnie this was *making* it big time.

"Many have called me that, but I prefer to think of myself as an entrepreneur on the seas." He smiled genuinely.

"Eric James." He said addressing me. "I've been reading about you in the papers. Very nice coos negotiating here and there." He smiled.

"Yes. Here and there." I responded with an acknowledged smile.

"And of course, your charming and most elegant wife." He took her hand and kissed it. Charlotte smiled back. I think she was chuckling inside.

"Raoul Estoya," he looked to his left, "this must be your lovely wife, Souetes. I have also seen you in the papers, especially followed that wonderful wedding a few years back. Quite a sensation." He stood for a moment and nodded. "And not to dismiss your studies on quantum physics. I have read several of your papers. Not sure I understand the true complexities but did enjoy the words and ideas." He smiled again. Souetes was smitten. A good looking man who actually read her papers. How rare.

"And I see you are current with the Social and Entertainment section." Raoul answered.

"Well you are all a hard act not to know." Again he smiled as he sipped. "And who might this lovely couple be?" He asked looking to Ross and Kathleen, extending a hand.

"Ross Hutchinson and his wife, Kathleen. Ross is in sugar. One of the largest sugar refineries - Redwing, I'm sure you've heard of it."

"And you, young man?" looking to Thornhill.

"He's with me. Company man." I answered quickly.

"And his friend?"

"An international spy." Ronnie answered.

"Now that does sound intriguing. We must talk." Aris said with a smile. The table laughed and the evening warmed up with dancing and foods and *safe* talk.

~ ~ ~ ~ ~ ~

~ I had thought the speech tonight had gone very well and it had been important that I include the segment on global business tactics. I had started with... "A fine line between espionage, spying and healthy competitive intelligence and economic gathering needs to be examined. The very words competitive intelligence serve to describe ethical and legal activities of systematically gathering, managing and analysing information on one's industrial competitors. It can be acquired by a number of means – newspaper articles, patent filings, information at trade shows, corporate publications, interviews by Humints -Human Intelligent gatherers - to determine information on a corporation, a thesis and even an idea. The gathering of information has been called CIS, Competitive Intelligence Solution or CRS, Competitive Response Solution. One might liken it to market research whereby an application of principles and practices is applied to the domain of global business. One might liken it to that of open-source intelligence. The fine line between that competitive intelligence and an economic or industrial espionage is not clear as one needs to recognize and understand the legal basics between the two.

"The border is often blurred and elusive as it is difficult sometimes to differentiate between legal and illegal methods of information gathering. Among those areas most targeted are engine technology, machine tools, materials, coatings, transportation, aviation, energy and the fast growing communications arena.

"IP, Intellectual Property, is a legal concept referring to creations of the mind that are given exclusive rights and are recognized as intangible assets. These could include artistic works such as literary, music or art itself, inventions and or discoveries and even certain phrases, words, symbols and design. These are then given copyrights, patents, tradedress, trademarks and in some cases they are called trade secrets. Industrial design rights covers the creation of shape, composition of pattern or colour, configurations and subsequent combinations of pattern and colour into additional dimensional forms containing aesthetic value, two and or three-dimensional patterns producing handicraft, industrial commodities or products. Trade secrets deal with a practice or specific design, instrument, pattern, process or any compilation of information not generally known, by which a business obtains its economic advantage over its customers and or competitors, whether it benefits a foreign country or especially for commercial and or economic purposes. Theft or misappropriation is a federal crime.

"As one can see this is a very complicated area with many gray areas and blurred fringes. I submit this information so that one can decide for one's self as to the case of espionage or simply clever outdoing of competitors." *And I thought **the close** strong and thought provoking. I had delivered a good night's work and it had been well received. The snow comforts as I drift. My mind thinks back to 1940. A great year with so much to offer. So much to accomplish.*

CHAPTER nine ~

It was late and the three of us had driven up to New York for the weekend. Charlotte and Souette were busy at a golf tournament in Beaconsfield, maybe not as glamorous but certainly star studded for the country club. All the top players had come in for a bit of R&R in Montreal and a quick segway to the Club became their usual stop off and our ladies Chaired the Club so it was 'show time'. Everyone loved the event.

Ronnie, Raoul and I stopped in after a nice dinner for a night cap. Billy Rose's Diamond Horseshoe was always a nice place to hang your hat and simply chill, especially if one were *in the area*, and we were. The management knew us well and treated us in a like-wise manner. We had taken a room at the Paramount so it was all on the property. No long walk home.

"Well look what the cat dragged in," Raoul said as he watched Aris, enter the room. "I guess the glamour of front page news has softened. The old boy's going it alone tonight. Shall we invite him over?"

"Absolutely." I smiled as I waved a hand in the air. "Aris. Come and join us." I shouted nicely.

He looked about, a bit disoriented at his name being bellowed out, then smiled and waved.

"Boys' night out is it?" He said joining us at the table.

"Apparently for all of us." Ronnie answered. "Take a seat, if you aren't expecting someone."

"Nice. And am not. Thanks." He took off his coat and put his

57

hat down. Always smart looking to a fault. He smiled a toothy grin.

"What are you all having?" He looked around as the cocktail waitress came over. "Give everyone the same and add a Manhattan. Thank you." He smiled looking up as he gave the order.

"So, what's the occasion that I find two married and one questionable male out on the town?" He said clasping both hands together as if in earnest.

"Just that. Out on the town. And you?" I answered.

"Needed to get away from the phone and the and the, if you get my drift." Again he smiled broadly. We all nodded.

"As good an answer as any." Ronnie offered. We all laughed and relaxed for a moment. Our drinks came and we saluted in unison then took a sip.

"So Aris, what's happening in the tanker business?" Ronnie ventured to break the silence.

"Getting paperwork completed while in port, before transporttation can begin." He said sipping quietly.

"Who's handling the paperwork?" I asked.

"Costas Bratanos in London. There are several foreign steamships tied up in Rio. Our first is to be held in both the Norwegian and Swedish shipyards, neutral flags. Cuts the high freight rates." He paused. "Freighters are the future of the war."

"Then you will corner the market I think." I said, with a smile and a raised glass. He nodded. I returned the nod.

"Costas a friend of yours, yes? And you can manage all from home base, here in New York?" Raoul asked.

"Yes. Long time." Aris answered. "And yes, here in New York."

"I believe you have interests in South America, am I right?" Raoul asked again.

"Yes." He replied then looking to me, "And I understand that your company, Eric, does too. Ammunition. Born of the explosives of Hamilton Powder. Parcel of the Defence Industries at CIL now. Am I not mistaken?"

"Quite right. We are all bedfellows in one way or another, like it or not, profit or not, neutral or not." I smiled back. He was a shrewd player.

Sweden had intelligence operations ongoing with the Allies

complete with espionage in Germany and listening stations in Sweden itself, not to mention military secret training headquarters for Norwegian and Danish soldiers. Sweden for all her neutrality was very active in the war game. Everyone was and everyone knew it.

It was interesting that Sections 5 and 13 of the Hague Convention 1907 dealt with the permanent neutral power as being a sovereign state bound by international treaty neutral towards belligerents of all wars, even future wars. Take Switzerland for example. This concept of neutrality in war was defined, narrowly, with constraints applied, on the neutral party in return for being internationally recognized as righted to remain neutral. Just looking at the Lateran Treaty of 1929 where Italy gave perpetual neutrality to the Pope in international relations giving way to abstention from mediation in controversy unless requested specifically by all parties. In short, the Vatican City will forever remain neutral ground. Belligerents ~ But enough. We were all out for some fun.

"Why don't we leave this establishment and head over to my apartment for a night cap?" The Greek offered.

"Fine idea indeed." I seconded. I pulled out my wallet and paid for the drinks plus tab then we all headed out. CIL was to enjoy this evening out with our friend, the man in tankers.

The evening was mild and yet brisk. Good for the head. I pulled up my coat collar and adjusted my hat. Charlotte had given it to me as a gift. It suited me and I relished wearing it. My mother had given me the kid gloves that always went with me. This was a wonderful reminder of her. We walked the few blocks chatting and looking at the building windows to the metro. It appeared we all enjoyed taking the underground rather than a cab.

Montreal, like all the large cities thinking ahead, had at one time considered a subway system. In fact, as early as 1902 there had been a concerted effort by MCTC (Montreal Central Terminal Co.) to actually open up both railways and roadways under the St. Lawrence River to the shore across the city itself, and run lines east, west, and north along the Island of Montreal but alas the debate and talk of it all simply raged on until a conclusion was met in 1910 stating that the project itself was of such magnitude that time was needed to fully analyse it further ~ the end resulted in work not actually begun until 1962 (of course, I was not to be *present* but my exhaustive efforts in furthering the project forward would not go unheeded, as I had had a hand in the those original plans which were to be used long after my temporal body was gone.) I smiled ~ something to be said for being a Time Traveling Functionary.

We exited near Beakman Place. Funny. Loved the name. Aris' apartment was anything but humble. It was stupendous by any standards. This he explained as being part of his façade. Good for business. We all smiled and headed to the bar. Some how things progressed from simple talk, business talk, feeling each other out as to ideology, to sex talk to undressing. Either we were all too drunk to be aware or we simply didn't care or we were just guys out on the town, without a care and obviously liked the company of each other.

Aris was a well-built man with broad shoulders and slender hips. He had taken a fancy to Ronnie and whether it was mutual or simply the Humint taking advantage of a situation, Ronnie took the bull by the horns and rode him enthusiastically. I will often think about that evening wondering about the SOE and Ronnie's duplicity in it. Special Operations Executive was officially formed by Hugh Dalton, Minister of Economic Warfare with the purpose to conduct sabotage, reconnaissance in occupied Europe and espionage to aid local resistance movements. It was top secret - few even knew of its existence. Baker Street Irregulars became the 'off' name due to its London headquarter location and sometimes called Churchill's Secret Army but to the inner circle the 'Ministry of Ungentlemanly Warfare'. Easily concealed by factious branch names – Air Ministry, War Office. The SOE operated in all countries including neutral territory. Out of the 13,000 employees almost 3200 were women. The SOE supported over 1,000,000 operatives worldwide. Ronnie's interest in the shipping magnet went far beyond his being amply well hung and playful.

CHAPTER ten ~

I met Huber Johnston the year Lily died. I was out on assignment in the UK and was invited to Marsh Court. I hadn't been back since the war days when I had been sent there to recuperate from injuries and to my delight I found myself pleasantly surprised to find that things hadn't changed much. Huber Johnston welcomed me as if a son returning from a long night's journey. At the time I didn't think it too odd but in retrospect I suppose it was. I was escorted to the basement through a maze of bookcases in the library that parted when a combination of books were pulled out as if building a tune that common folk were not privy to hear. The bookcase separated and a passage way revealed itself. The man in dark brown escorted me down a flight of stairs. Endlessly long flight it seemed, maybe two or three landings below ground. I was later to learn that there were ten floors below that ~ a Command Base basement. Headquarters for a highly organized network, a worldwide network that kept tabs and acquired all manner of information pertaining to secret projects. It was the hub central for industrial espionage – worldwide. Headed by Huber himself. It was, in and of itself, an underground ultra modern building with hybrid plants, labs and equipment – state of the art – some of the smartest minds on the planet – from where world decisions were being made on a daily basis, where land was divvied up, population survival balanced against the pros and cons, their fate, Earth's fate, all resting in the hands of a group of internationally chosen men sitting around a table. They were known as the EPPA (Earth Provisional Protection Agency). Skin coats. People wearing identities that were surface only. *I would become one ~ one of the men. One who would know too much. Perhaps.*

 I was then blindfolded and told to stand quietly. I was not sure what any of this had to do with my being summoned to Marsh Court by a man I had met so many years ago. It was soon clear that it was the beginning of my initiation into the brotherhood and it was at the request of my sponsor that I had been invited.

 Huber Johnston was that sponsor unbeknownst to me. In order to join the fraternity a man must ask to join that fraternity as he will not be solicited but he also must be sponsored. I was later to find out about his relationship with my mother, dear Lily, for which I give thanks for his connection thereof.

 I am not at liberty to say anything about the actual ceremony, but that it was that, filled with pomp and circumstance, fire and brimstone and many pledges. I would wear my ring with great pride throughout my life. And thanks to the benevolent society my career accelerated quickly. My business contacts were expanded and those connections led me to places and deals that might not otherwise have been available. But that is not something I can attest to as I had been on the road for some time. The added boost was not to be dismissed though. I relished every bit of aid I could get ~ always have. Lily taught me well.

As to the origins of the fraternal organization they can actually be traced back to stonemasons. Craft labour was known as Operative Freemasonry. Lodges, incorporations and craft guilds. Two of the principle tools found at these lodges were the square and compass, as in Masons' "squaring their actions by the square of their virtue" and learning to "circumscribe their desires and keep their passions within due bounds toward all mankind." But being a non-dogmatic organization, interpretation is open as to what the words or symbols refer to. But charitable and community service activities are of prime interest. Money is collected only from the membership then distributed to various charities. These charities can be outside - non-Masonic on the world /global arena. Homes, sheltering homes, educational grants as in the Royal Masonic School (UK) open to everyone, medical assistance, CHIP (Masonic Child Identification Programs), the Masonic Service Association, Shriners Hospital for Children, and Masonic Medical Research Laboratory are just among a few of their interests. Many and varied.

Early Freemasons were not indentured servants or serfs but rather free men, so they travelled about openly. Those involved in the erection of cathedrals and monasteries were given a tax franchise which freed them from government control. And hence, in France, gave rise to the term "franc-macon" and "frère macon". We have called ourselves 'brother' for well over three hundred years and the bond amongst us has remained strong suggesting that important social needs were being met. Are being met.

And as to my mother's involvement with Huber it was all part of her history, our history.

Apparently as children, Huber Johnston didn't live far from Lily in the Northern part of UK. They met when her father was called in to work a horse in the neighbourhood. It was then that they became friends. They were both fourteen. As Huber came from means and Lily not, nothing could ever have come from their relationship. Lily later married and moved to Bradford. Huber was a young man on the rise and as he was to visit the city, our city, he stayed at the Victoria, the same hotel where I and my buddy would work. It was there that Huber gave Lily the bracelet which I in turn gave to Charlotte as a gift from my mother. It was Huber's gift *in friendship* and with that went a promise to watch out for her and hers. And he did. With my father dead, times were tight. Huber paid our family's travel to America and he paid for the house in NDG. I'm not sure that Eric, my father, would have liked that another man was responsible for the welfare of his wife but I do know he would not have begrudged Lily her chance to make a name for herself. Bradford was a hard town for a woman alone with three children. I think my father smiles down, always watching.

I digress. The Canadian Meeting. Huber is eighty-five and healthy. He is wielding power still. It is 1940. Petroleum is now in great demand becoming the most valuable commodity traded on world markets. Canada has become an energy giant, an essential element as world supplier. Petroleum is the raw material for chemical products, plastics, solvents, and fertilizers ~ all the common petro chemical classes being olefins and aromatics, the very building blocks for polymers, fibbers, adhesives, lubricants and gels.

Edwin Drake began the first modern drilling company in 1859 in West Virginia and Pennsylvanian, so by the 1920s, oil fields were springing up globally ~ Sweden, Poland, Ukraine, Peru, Canada, Venezuela and the States. But product needed to be transported so Ludvig Nobel in Sweden 1878 took on the task. He built the Zoroaster, the first oil tanker, which operated from Baku to Astrakhan. This revolutionized oil transport and with that the kerosene lamp's popularity refined industry. Interestingly within a few years time, Canada would start constructing the vast pipeline network. Canadian exports of natural gas becomes second to that of Russia, as Canada is home to the world's largest natural gas liquids extraction facility.

Aris Nassi was on time. His Arinton was housed in the Swedish shipyards. His tankers, his fleet, sailed under neutral flags (Sweden, Panama) in efforts to exploit the high freight taxes. And with his connections all in place, he was riding high. As I said before, he had interests in South America as did our ammunition, after all, CIL was part and parcel of the Defence Industries, having been born out of the explosives of Hamilton Powder. Europe and the Americas. Mexico

included. Aris had subscripted his old friend Costas Bratnos, based in London, to buy up foreign steamships tied up in Rio. Aris Nassi was a very shrewd player. I had to give him credit. And with Souettes'
South American 'family of friends' and Raoul's Mexican connections, and Thornhill and Ronnie as aiders, Aris' business was growing. Huber talked about the Greek's tankers, the oil, the natural gas ~ endless needs, and all the while I seemed to be central in one way or another to all the players. My players. They were all my players.

Suddenly the night sky comes down and flashes before me, taking my breath away with a sharp slap. The snow is very cold then hot against my cheek. Time to go. I fade ~ whispering.

~ ~ ~ ~

Come Full Round Again
The Passage of time ~

Old Montreal / Vieux Montreal was once again looking at a new landscape. Time has a way of expanding and contracting on a whim, a fragile balance on the spin of a dime. Einstein said that if you ran fast enough you would meet yourself at the start. I will be at the start, the start of something new, soon. *I have lived a very long time* I thought to myself recalling those same words written in my father's memorial. He was quoted. And yet somehow I never thought he was referring to corporeal time. I have been sitting here enjoying the cool air, crunching the bits of crusty snow under the heel of my boot, slowly moving it rhythmically back and forth on the ground. The Holiday lights infuse Old Montreal with an enchantment that almost glows.
This is the park, a series of benches with flowers and grasses on either side dividing the walk, the long walk paths now under the Holiday snows, that Brandt and I had envisioned when we first under-

took to change and expand the landscape of Vieux Montreal, the waterfront that has now become home to so many, both visiting and those staying. The dock area well west of the archaeological site of Pointe a Calliere now stands as an urbanized jungle of shops and social venues, nicely tempered with bee friendly landscaping and an eco friendly atmosphere for all. The Chamber of Commerce had once again approached me, begging me out of retirement, a state I had entered into long after Charlie's death. Their offer was so enticing that it was a no-brainer, as my daughter, Grace, had said. Not only to be part of the planning itself but a shareholder in that stake itself. Thirty years have passed. I am now longer active though I retain a place on the board. My input is still of worth, it appears, as a visual testament. And although age is in the eye of the beholder, in truth, I think they like to have an *original* to roll out for occasional show. I am now ninety-seven. I am double the age my daughter Grace was when I started the project and double my own age when I started to unpack the boxes. Brandt and I moved here into our penthouse after I put the boxes filled with unanswered questions away, filing them in a safe place along with their key, in hopes that maybe another interested party might be able to unravel the locked mysteries of the man from Yorkshire. I hoped Emillio, my grandson, might. But I doubt I will live to see or ever know if he does. No matter.

    I love the look of our building. It was well ahead of its time thirty years ago, *modern age* as contrasted to the rich gray stone buildings of the original dwellers of Hachalago, Montreal. And I guess I too, have retained a modicum of grace and style. Two old dames down on the waterfront.

    "What are you smiling about dear?" Brandt had asked as he looked up, taking a sip of his drink. Neat.

    "I was just thinking how we all got here, at this point in time. Life certainly has been an interesting journey." I paused. "Don't you think dear?" I asked looking at him. I saw him in my mind's eye and for a moment the chill in the night air was warmed by the visual of the cosy fireplace and the fresh scent of pine needles from our Holiday fir tree. I shook the small flakes that were now floating down ever so gently. I held my hand out and watched them hit my gloves, some to rest and remain, others to flash melt in an instant. Life encapsulated.

    Brandt had been such a handsome man with a wonderful

smile. We had weathered well together. Together in our later years. Odd to have found someone so long after Charlie and so well into my life. But I did not question it and neither had he. Brandt. A tall interesting European who was himself an architect and spearhead of the *then new* ground breaking project, who had charmed the City into creating a revitalization of the dock front along the St. Lawrence River. Such another lifetime ago it seems.

We had met at the founders initial meeting where we discussed what was to be. I enjoyed his straightforward approach. He always cut to the chase yet never dismissed. He was the main financial support and from his past history very successful. He had been a Mason, like my father, and connected to Huber Johnston through his father. Indeed a small world and all interconnected in so many ways. Brandt and I combined our passion for building and the love of life, as people in our then early sixties come to better appreciate. And over the years we had weathered the storms that blew over and enjoyed the sun that had continued to shine. Brandt would have been ninety- eight this month. Two peas in a pod. He'd enjoyed a good lease on life, as he phrased it. And indeed, I agreed. We both had.

"You sound as though it's coming to an end. Is it?"

"I certainly hope not. Too many things yet to do, places to go and people to see." I gestured to the world about us.

"Now that sounds like my gal. We do have tickets for a flight in a few weeks. I would hate to miss that."

"Don't think we will."

"Good. Emillio would hate to miss the adventure."

I smiled to myself. Emillio. My grandson. Such a clever young man. I always took such delight in these little escapes from reality. But then who determines what is real and what isn't. And for a moment I lifted my head to the open sky above and heard the night music filling the penthouse room as George entered with a snack to nibble on before dinner.

"How kind George. Thank you."

"Thought you might like a bite to stave off the hunger." He smiled as he backed out. He was such old school and delightfully so.

George stayed on long after Brandt passed away. Brandt and I did make the last trek with Emillio and it was grand. I haven't been on an outing since, other than local treks along the waterfront and to museums. The loss of Brandt took its toll.

    I rubbed my hands together to bring myself back to today, to this moment, the now, the evening, the lights, the crunchy snow, the floating flakes, and soft whispering breeze. George would have dinner fixed shortly and a good hot toddy awaited. I always enjoyed the orderliness that George orchestrated my life around, giving it space and time to breathe and yet continuity. My faculties were very much in tact, perhaps a bit short on quick recall now and then, but always there for the important issues at hand. Sadly though my body was not as sound as it had been when I was eighty. The skis had long since been packed away. But I still walk with George or by myself as everyone knows me and I feel quite safe and watched over, as it were. I do walk slower and use my father's cane, a cane, which my mother Charlotte had given him on one of his birthdays stating that a gentleman without a walking stick was *less than*. I always smile when I think of that and that thought itself gives me solace. My, how far the man from Yorkshire had gone in his life. TTF. Never did understand what that meant. I even asked Brandt once but he simply shook his head. Maybe Huber Johnston might have known. A Mason thing perhaps.

    The breeze picks up a bit. It is soft and somehow warm riding on that chilled night air. There is a whispering murmur in it. I strain as if to hear the voice, as indeed it is a voice I hear. I think maybe the sounds of a conversation from somewhere out on the pathway but then realize it isn't. It is the breeze itself whispering. Whispering in a voice that I know but have not heard since I was a child.

    Suddenly I feel a presence. I am aware that a small figure is approaching me from the left side. I watch the snow being swished away in total abandonment. It is refreshing. Thoughts of my childhood playing in large leaf piles, hay stacks and snow drifts. I watch as the figure comes closer. It is a child in a long trench coat and rubbers.

    Then I hear, "Hello Miss James."

    My mouth unexpectedly goes dry. Nobody has called me that since I was a child, certainly not since I was an adult, eons ago. How would a child know my name, my maiden name? I brace myself, sitting up straighter on the bench, planting my feet solidly on the ground, gripping my hands into the bench seat to steady myself.

    "Who calls my name?" I ask.

"The wind." The child answers. It was a small boy, not older than seven, with rosy cheeks and curly hair.
"The wind?" I ask. "What kind of response is that?" I challenge. He stands in front of me, motionless. There is nothing frightening or menacing. We simply look at each other in silence.
"The truth Miss James. I was told to give you a message, if I might?"
"By whom?"
"If I might Miss James." He said, pausing, waiting for permission. I nod. He bent forward and whispered into my ear.
And for some strange reason I close my eyes as I listen to the sound of the gentle whisper, a whisper from the breeze. A whisper that has been carried through the ages. I smile. We have come full round and the answers to oh so many questions are made clear. Clear in that split second from a whisper on the breeze in my ear by a strange child on that snowy night. I open my eyes and find myself alone. There is no one standing near. No sign of foot steps in the snow by the bench or along the path. No sign of anyone in the park but myself. Alone. Silent. With a warm breeze whispering.

    I took a deep breath and smiled contentedly. I raised myself from the bench and inhaled deeply taking in the night air. I pulled my scarf up around my ears, patted my gloves together and then started toward my apartment where George would be waiting with something warm and decidedly tasty. But suddenly the night sky came down and flashed before me, taking my breath away with a sharp slap. My legs buckled slowly as if in slow motion and I gently fell to the ground. I felt no pain, no fear, nothing. The voice in the breeze sang to me, gently, soothingly. I felt the cold snow on my cheek and then with a heavy sigh I slipped silently into the dark to join the whisper on the breeze.

Other books:

BOOTS AND PEARLS,
DIARY OF CITYGAL BEEKEEPER
Revisited 2015

A TIME FOR GRACE
TICK TOCK

TWISTED LIVES WICKED LIES

THE MAN FROM YORKSHIRE

FRANKIE and FRIENDS (series)
VOODOO WHISPERS (bk1)
DOUBLE DENSITY, CHILD OF THE MIST (bk2)
HIDDING IN PLAIN SIGHT (bk3)

5 PARKSIDE PLACE

THE OCCUPATIONAL TOURIST

PABLO HASEN-PFEFFER

DARK FOREST

STRICTLY CONDIFENTIAL

with more to come ~

Printed in Great Britain
by Amazon